LUMBERJILL

Escape from
Younish

TYLER H. JOLLEY • MARY H. GEIS

JOLLEY
CHRONICLES

To all my readers who aren't afraid to roll up
their sleeves and work hard in life.

For my best friends and sisters, Jessica and Trista.
I love you.

CHAPTER 1

The curious pile of wet, rotten leaves captured my attention as I tried to catch my breath. The rain had stopped, but the ground remained saturated. My chest heaved. Lungs burned. Running had become difficult. My legs felt like two hunks of wood. The only thing keeping them moving was the jolt of pain from the forest floor on my bare feet. What *was* under that mound of leaves? A carcass of a rodent? The forgotten skeleton of a betrayer? Maybe even treasure meant to be hidden in the forest? Perhaps nothing at all. Regardless of what lay beneath, it calmed my nerves and gave me something else to focus on.

Breathe, I told myself over and over. Hyperventilation gripped my chest as I sprinted and my breath came in quick, unsatisfying spurts. I was in good shape, but my mind was betraying my body. *Get it together, Annalise.*

A cold wind gust bit my skin and whipped my long blond hair around my face. I swiped it behind my ears. The pile of leaves had blown away. Moonlight exposed the barren ground below. As I examined the empty ground, another sharp blast of air whisked me back to reality.

I had to run. I was already this far in. A faint orange

glow of torches followed me. Distant. But close enough to catch me. They were closing in fast.

I tucked my hair into the nape of my white nightgown and sprinted. Fallen branches stabbed at my feet as I sprinted. I didn't know where I was headed, but it didn't matter. As long as it was away from Younish Camp.

My home.

There was no going back now. Not with the new rules in place. When the Scrawn Law was enacted, I'd been in denial. Complete disbelief. There was no way anyone could enforce the harsh rules. Lumberchief Paul was crazy for introducing it in the first place.

I'd ignored it until tonight. That was the first time they'd enforced the heinous law. It was cold and raining. Clouds had insulated and magnified the blood-curdling screams of both mother and baby. The lumberchief had been so cavalier about the whole thing. Perhaps that was the most disturbing part. "The suckling has been released," he had announced to the crowd.

I'd seen more than my mind could process. I had wandered around camp aimlessly for a few minutes trying to gather myself. Then I saw the distraught mother being led away. Two lumberjack mechanicals held her up, their grafted appendages digging into her arms. She could barely stand, let alone walk. Despite the cold, her clothes clung to her from sweat. Her hair was matted to her tearstained face. From the waist down, her nightgown was stained with blood. Perhaps she was going to be released as well—I wasn't sure. I hadn't cared to find out.

She had locked eyes with me for just a moment—a look of desperation and fear was painted on her face— then she was dragged away. At first, I didn't realize I was even running. Not until I heard someone calling after me.

But even then, it sounded so distant. As if they were yelling at me through water.

Like a thief in the night, I escaped the wall of Younish Camp.

* * *

The bile in the back of my throat was impossible to ignore any longer. I leaned against a tree and tried to compose myself, but the feeling didn't pass. I sucked in a deep breath—the smell of fresh pine used to be a scent I welcomed. But tonight, my whole body heaved as I returned my dinner to the earth. My ribs ached as I emptied the meager contents of my stomach.

Then I heard it.

The whirr of a chainsaw interrupted the sickness.

Mechanicals. The men of my camp.

No, no, this can't be. How did they catch up so quickly?

I stood slowly and scanned the area. The torches were closer now, and I could make out the silhouettes of the mechanicals.

They were all grafted in one way or another, a way to distinguish themselves from the purist lumberjacks. That was their initiation. Some had chainsaws where arms once were, others had saws for legs—even hammers grafted atop their heads wasn't unheard of.

I scrambled forward, almost losing my footing, and ran. My life depended on it.

Brush clawed at my nightgown and branches scratched my arms. It didn't matter. I had to get to the next camp over. Where I might be safe. The clang of metal rang in my ears. Closer by the second.

I thought of what'd I say at the gates of Crempshaw

Camp. As I rehearsed my plea for help in my head, I suddenly realized I was no longer running, and my face smacked against the cold dirt.

I shook the cobwebs from my head as stabbing pain radiated up my leg. I sat up and pushed myself against a large boulder. Warm blood ran down my leg and trickled between my toes. I gingerly bent my leg so I could get a closer look at my injury.

A branch had speared my calf muscle. In one side and out the other. No time to stop. The chainsaws were no more than a hundred yards away. Forcing myself to my feet, I took one step and found myself on the ground again with my hand covering my mouth. Panic coursed through my veins. I bit my lip and pulled the branch until it was free from one side. Blood gushed, covering the leafed floor.

I should have left it in. Now I was stuck with it in one side while the other side bled like a stuck pig.

Fire burned up my entire leg when I attempted to continue my escape. The sound of hammers breaking rocks, axes assaulting branches, and chainsaws destroying saplings filled the chaotic air. There was no way to outrun them anymore.

I used my arms and one good leg to crawl to a fallen tree. Pine needles shredded my skin. My useless leg throbbed with each movement.

The whirr of a chainsaw was mere yards away. Hiding was my only option. I'd left a breadcrumb trail of blood behind me, and the rate at which I was hemorrhaging was alarming. But I banked on the nightfall to hide my tracks.

I leaned against the tree, panting heavily; my head rested against the rough, sticky bark. I closed my eyes and gripped the bottom of my filthy nightgown. Pulling as hard as I could in a linear motion, I tore a large strip off my gown. With shaky hands, I bent my knee on the offending leg and placed the material around the upper portion of my calf.

I dipped my chin down and bit on the yoke of my top, then pulled and knotted the material tight around my muscle. My vision blurred for a second, but my scream was muffled, and the tourniquet was in place. I might lose a leg, but I wouldn't bleed to death tonight.

A mechanical, with axes for legs, hobbled by too closely. He used his leg to chop at a tree. *Bang. Bang. Bang.* The ground vibrated with each smack. I'd gone unnoticed in the cover of the night, but I needed to be better hidden. Animal instinct kicked in; I burrowed deep into the leaves. In the end, I was covered. I peered through the rotting leaves and saw them rapidly approaching.

"Annalise, we're coming for you!" a mechanical taunted. "You can't outrun us, scrawn."

A mechanical with a hammer grafted to the top of his head dragged a rock into the clearing. "I can't wait to get my hands on you. Or should I say, head on you?" He arched his back, paused for a second, then thrust forward as if his spine were a loaded spring. Sparks and rock shards exploded around the clearing. An owl hoot echoed in the forest. The deranged men of my camp would stop at nothing.

"Let's get her," another one yelled. He used his ax arms to chop down a tree three feet from me. I flinched with the fall.

Each one left a personalized stamp of ruin on the area. Then it all stopped. Lumberjacks were great listeners. And tonight, amongst all the chaos and destruction, a sound pricked their ears. I heard it too. It sent icy chills down my back. Far in the distance, a keringer howled.

"If you know what's good for you, you'll come back

home," a mechanical said. He laughed like a maniac. "We'll be gentler than the keringer."

The lumberjack mechanicals grouped together in hushed whispers.

"Last chance, scrawn!"

The keringer bellowed again. I couldn't make out which direction it was coming from.

Without another word, they receded into the forest. Leaving me alone. They got to go back to the warm fire and keringer-proof walls of Younish.

I stayed motionless, too terrified to move. Out of options. Maybe if I closed my eyes, it would all go away? Like a horrible nightmare. My vision blurred again; I didn't fight it this time.

When I came to, the howling had stopped. I had to get help. The tourniquet had to be removed before I lost my leg. My home was the enemy's camp now. The lumberjacks at Younish would never welcome me again.

I was screwed.

CHAPTER 2

Pain was the only thing keeping me awake. My chest heaved and my breath curled from inside me. White and visible. The mechanicals were long gone. Or perhaps they'd found something more interesting to hunt than a scrawn like me.

I gingerly lifted my leg to examine my wound. It still oozed blood. I didn't know what to do. Should I still try to hobble to Crempshaw Camp? I wasn't sure how much farther it was, but I did know my own camp was only a few miles back. Would Crempshaw even take me like this? Just six feet tall, I was average height. But I was strong, and my broad shoulders were bigger than most of the female breeders. But now, showing up with a branch sticking out of my leg, and a blood-soaked nightgown, what was I supposed to say? *Hi, I'm Annalise of Younish Camp, Lumberchief Paul has lost his freaking mind and I need to shack up here, okay? Oh, that thing sticking out of my leg? Can you fix that? And feed me? And house me? One more thing: I won't be able to contribute jack for at least a week or two. That's providing I don't lose my leg.* Yeah, I doubted they'd take on such a burden.

I pressed my balled fists against my forehead and fought the urge to scream. I knew what I had to do. Even if it was just until I was healed. I had to sneak back to

Younish and recover. It was a big enough camp—the biggest in the area. Maybe I could conceal myself until I was better?

I'm such an idiot!

Hot tears streamed down my face. My head flopped back and rested against a tree. I wiped my dirty face with the back of my hands and tried to get my bearings. Despite the clouds above me, I could still make out the moon and North Star. I readied myself to make the journey back on unsteady feet.

Each step felt like having a hot poker shoved up my heel. The few miles back to camp suddenly felt impossible. Blood trickled steadily down my leg. The tourniquet had loosened. This was going much worse than I'd envisioned. Lifting a three-hundred-pound tree trunk? No problem. Clean the disgusting men's quarters in record time? You bet! Making a successful plan? Nope, not me. Just call me Failure-lise.

A rustle in the trees stole my attention. I paused and looked around wildly. A large plume of fog puffed into the air, quickly followed by the deep bellow of the beast hidden in the trees.

The keringer.

How was I so stupid? In my panic and self-loathing, I hadn't even thought about the keringer. I cursed under my breath. Outrunning a keringer with a healthy body was immensely lucky, but with a serious injury? I might as well have built a fire and roasted myself. Everyone deserved a hot dinner, right?

I carefully ducked behind a tree and waited. Each step shook the ground as it stalked toward my direction.

Ice ran in my veins.

Its heavy strides paused for a moment. The clouded moon provided little light, but I was still able to see its outline. Large wings attached to a bear-like body. Except instead of thick hair, it was sparse and coarse.

Crap.

It was a male keringer.

His pace quickened and he began to trot, his tongue licking the air, following a scent. *My* scent. It brushed past me. Wiry hairs scraped against my bare arm. I gasped. My hiding spot from the mechanicals was now being invaded by the keringer. Its thick tongue greedily licked the blood puddle I had so graciously left behind. An appetizer.

I cautiously limped over branches and stepped on only bare soil, avoiding noisy branches and leaves. This was my only chance to get away. Hopefully, my blood was enough to satisfy its midnight snack, but I knew better. Right now, I was an injured seal and he was a shark.

But none of that mattered. I had to tiptoe quietly. Impaled leg be damned. Wind whipped hair across my face. My chest heaved. One foot in front of the other. Quickly. Stealthily. I could cry later. Besides, he wasn't the only keringer out there.

Once the adrenaline rush of fear had passed, I stood and my vision clouded, and I stumbled. How much blood had I lost? My foot was completely soaked. I left crimson footprints with each step.

Finally, I saw the orange glow in the distance.

My camp. My prison.

CHAPTER 3

The large bonfire in the center of Younish filled me with both hope and terror. At least I could stop and rest. I made my way to the back side of camp near the tents, away from the main entrance.

Tall, sharpened trees surrounded the camp. They'd used only the tallest and strongest ones when they constructed the perimeter. What they didn't know was my lover had made a small hole in the back where he and I could sneak in and out of camp. To my knowledge, it was the only breach in the walls and was well hidden. My chest tightened when I thought of him.

I took a deep breath and pushed my messy blonde hair behind my ears. The throbbing in my leg had become worse by the second. I placed a shaky hand against a spire and lowered myself to the cold, damp ground. Exhaustion slammed into me as dusk broke the horizon. Every muscle trembled, my breath came in short spurts, and if not for the incredible pain throbbing in my leg, I would have passed out an hour ago. I had to find a place to hide before daylight.

I crawled, dragging my useless leg behind me. Finally, a gap presented itself. Sideways was the only way I would fit. I shimmied in until the branch in my leg halted my progress and caught on the gap. Silent screams raged through my body. Hot tears moistened my flushed cheeks. I rested on my back and stared at the fading stars. Once composed, I twisted my leg and pulled it through the opening.

Marshall, I thought. I had to find Marshall. He was my closest friend, and he might help me. Or turn me in. At this rate, I wasn't clinging to hope or luck, since the only kind I had was bad. But it was the only chance I had, and that was something.

I staggered past the mess hall, which really wasn't a hall at all. More like an open-air structure lined with long tables. I hobbled into the kitchen; a small lantern barely illuminated the area. Although I could only see his back, I knew it was him. Marshall. His short, tight, brown curls were still wet from his morning shower. He was only a few inches taller than me, and had he been a woman, he wouldn't have been considered scrawn. But at six foot three, he was too small, and he'd never be a breeder. He could work, but not breed. His lineage would stop with him. Always dutiful, he was the only one up and preparing breakfast for the entire camp.

"Marsh—" I cleared my throat as tears bubbled up. I buried them down deep, where they belonged. "Marshall."

His spine stiffened and he stilled. He turned only his head in my direction. "Annalise?" He dropped an egg and rushed to my side. "Annalise, I thought . . . they . . . the mechanicals, they said you died."

I wrapped my arm around his shoulder, easing the weight off my leg. "Well, it wasn't from lack of effort on my own part. Those idiots walked right past me."

"What happened? You look terrible."

"This?" I pointed to the impaled, blood-soaked branch. "Did that all on my own." I tried to laugh but it came out as a cough. "I'm not sure, Marsh, but one minute I was running, the next I was kissing the ground and this branch was making love to my leg. You always said I had nice legs, right?"

He led me to a chair and knelt down. "Annalise"—he examined my leg—"you're really hurt. And you're as pale as a ghost. How much blood did you lose?"

"The regular amount."

"This is serious. We need to hide you. They think you're dead."

I stared at Marshall's mouth, but the words seemed far away. The room spun and the pain in my leg was fading.

"Now," was the last thing I heard before I felt Marshall scoop me up and the world turned black.

CHAPTER 4

I lay there, beckoning my eyes to open, but they refused; pine sap and tea tree oil stung my nostrils. And then I was out again. Struggling to wake up but not succeeding. I played this little game for who knew how long.

Suddenly, I sat straight up, and the scent of pine sap was replaced by burning flesh. *My* burning flesh.

"Pmhf da pha!" I tried to yell, but a cloth had been shoved in my mouth.

"Shh," Marshall whispered. "I have to cauterize your leg. I couldn't get it to stop bleeding. I'm so sorry, Annalise. Take a deep breath. I'm not done."

I felt the searing poker press against my skin again. Turned out that feeling of having a hot poker in my heel before was nothing compared to the real thing. My back arched in protest and I passed out.

* * *

"What the hell, Marshall? Where am I?"

"Keep your voice down." Marshall sat on a chair next to my bed. "You almost bled to death, I think. I had to cauterize both sides of your leg. I've been changing the bandage and cleaning it. You should be okay, but it'll be a few days before you'll have full use of it. Drink this, you've been out nearly an entire day."

"Great." I drained the water from the glass. The cool water rushing down my throat felt like aloe on a sunburn. "Then I'll be out of here."

"Where are you going to go, Annalise?"

"Crempshaw Camp. I'm not staying here. Not with the Scrawn Law." I ran my fingers through my hair. "I hate Paul!"

"Lumberchief Paul is your brother," he said.

"Exactly. Could he even make an exemption for his own sister? Hell, no."

"It's not that bad."

"Yes, it is," I replied.

"Okay, the food rations are not ideal for the scrawn. But it's livable."

"No, it's not." I folded my arms across my broad chest.

"Stop being unreasonable."

"I'm not."

"It's not like you're pregnant."

I stared at him flatly.

"Anna, no." He stood abruptly and the chair toppled over. "No, no, no. How?"

I raised an eyebrow.

"Who?"

"Do either of those factors really matter? Besides, the father is out of the picture." I tried to stand and immediately regretted it. Despite sleeping the day away, I was starting to feel weak and tired. I grimaced and lowered myself back onto the cot. "No. My fate, and every pregnant scrawn's fate, is sealed, thanks to my dear brother."

"I . . ." He trailed off. "Do you know how, um, how far along you are?"

I shrugged. "I don't know. Maybe three or four months? I'm not sure, but I've had a ton of nausea and time really isn't on my side right now. I have to leave."

"Do you have any clue how far Crempshaw is?"

"Five, six miles?"

"Try over one hundred."

My eyes widened.

"Guess I really didn't plan that out well, did I?"

"What was your plan anyway? To get killed?"

"Get off my case, Marshall. I just kinda freaked out. After the baby was released, I had to get out of there. Here. I don't know. Ugh, stupid Paul. This is all his fault."

"Wait," Marshall said slowly. "He's not the . . . I mean, he's not—"

"Sick! No, of course not. The Scrawn Law is his fault, you sicko."

Marshall paced across the floor, kicking up dirt. "We'll figure something out. There's food on the tray next to you. Eat."

"I'll just throw it up. The whole pregnancy thing is no joke. Honestly, I'm surprised I haven't thrown up the baby." I laughed, but behind it, I was terrified.

"Well, I'll bring you something for that. Eat your dinner and rest. I'll figure something out in the morning." He righted the chair, sat down, and took my hands into his own. "And for the love of everything that is good, please be quiet and stay put until we have a plan."

I nodded but said nothing.

"Anna, I mean it. I can't let anything else happen to you."

"Fine. But the second I can walk, I'm leaving. And I'm taking the women with me. All of them."

CHAPTER 5

Once again, pine sap and tea tree oil were my alarm clock. The cobwebs in my head weren't as thick as the day before. With heavy eyelids, I stared at the unfamiliar surroundings.

I'd heard of junk drawers before, but this was an entire junk room. Discarded and leftover parts from mechanicals lined one canvas wall; broken and rusted axes, chainsaws, and clamps lined the other. The sour scent of mildew replaced the heady oils used to heal my leg. Black mold was thick and weaved its way in and out of the canvas folds. The tent was as rotten as strawberries in September.

A flap caught in the breeze, and I saw a figure fill the void. I burrowed deep into the warm wool covers, trying to hide from the intruder.

"Annalise, it's me."

"Marshall?" I sat up quickly and almost knocked the cot over. "Where am I? This place is a dump."

"It's the parts room."

"Was I here yesterday?"

"Yes, you didn't notice? You were pretty out of it. And combative." He placed a wooden tray on the lopsided table. "For you."

"It stinks."

He furrowed his brow. "I'm sorry. I just, I thought you'd be hungry."

"Oh." I shook my head. "Not the food. The room, it reeks. This is the place where mold comes to multiply and die." I cupped the warm bowl and breathed in steam. Salty broth coated my throat as I greedily gulped it. "Thank you for the bone broth, Marsh. I'm starving."

"I'll sneak you some more a little later. With your *condition*, we'll have to be extra careful."

I pushed myself to my feet. "What condition? I'm great." I grimaced.

Marshall pointed to my leg. "Not that condition." He nodded his head, staring at my abdomen. "*That*."

"Right." I sat and pulled my knees to my chest. "That's a little more complicated than a sliced calf. Speaking of which, I'd like to get out of here."

"And go where?" Marshall shook his head.

"I told you, Crempshaw. It's clean, no typhoid or dysentery, and *no* mechanicals. They're downstream from the mountain runoff so they get first pick at the best water. Oh, and some crazed, narcissistic psychopath isn't running the show."

"How do you know all of that propaganda you've heard is true?"

"Because Paul is a one-of-a-kind nightmare."

"Anna." He paced. "You know what I mean."

"It can't be worse than here. You've seen the papers; only good news comes out of Crempshaw. And that brings me to my next point." I shoved a pieced of crusty bread in my mouth. "I meant what I said. I want to take everyone. All the women, scrawn or not, need out of this place. Same with anyone else who wants to defect."

"You're almost as crazy as your brother." Marshall rubbed his hands over his face. "And how do you propose that? The lumberchief sent an entire party after you, a single scrawn. What makes you think you can take a large portion of the group?"

I shrugged. "Well, I'm not going to ask for permission. I'll sneak them out. I dunno? Come on, Marsh, you know we're all on death row here. We can figure something out."

"We?"

"Huh." I stood and groaned. Stupid leg. "Forget it. Never mind." I took a step toward the door and pointed. "Just stay out of my way, then."

Marshall grabbed my hand and walked me toward the canvas cot. The morning sun hadn't warmed up the dirt yet. Cold shivers ran from my feet to my head. Then, the nausea that had plagued me for the last few months reared its sickening head. I gripped Marshall's thick forearm with my left hand, turned, and retched away from us. My ribs ached, my throat burned, and my blue eyes bulged.

My feet were swept up, and I found myself in Marshall's arms. He walked evenly and gently deposited my embarrassed, cold, and tired body on the bed. As if to remind me I had even bigger problems than my expanding belly, my leg started trickling warm blood. Marshall cursed and rummaged in a leather bag.

He positioned a three-legged stool next to me and guided my leg off the edge. "Annalise, I want to help. I do." His eyes seemed desperate or sad. I couldn't quite tell, but it made me feel horrible. All the trouble he'd gone through in the last two days was risky, enough to have him publicly executed if Paul found out. Marshall applied pressure on my loose scab. "We have to proceed with great caution. And a better plan, a *real* plan. But first, you must heal."

He was right. "Dang it, Marshall," I said. "Fine. Just

give me a day or two and I'll be good as new. I mean, look how much better I am already. My body was meant for this. I was probably a warrior in a past life." I grinned.

"There's more," he started. "There was chatter at breakfast. It seems Lumberchief Paul was unsatisfied with the reports of your killing. No body, no death. He didn't believe his henchmen and made an example out of one this morning. He confessed, but it was too late for him. Paul knows you're still alive."

I pushed his hand off me and held the pressure on my own. Teabags inside the rag helped clot the wound, but my fingers were quickly coated with thick, sticky blood. My stomach lurched but I swallowed hard.

"So . . ." Marshall paced again and suddenly found great interest in the floor. This wasn't going to be good. "I just think we need to reintegrate you into the group."

"Are you nuts?"

"It'll buy us some time to figure out how to make our escape. I can't keep you in here much longer. They use this tent on occasion; you're bound to get caught."

"Okay." The bleeding stopped, so I lay back on my cot. "I'm so sure crazy-pants Paul will have no problem with me, a fugitive scrawn who also happens to be his pregnant sister, limping back into camp. He'll probably welcome me with open arms. Arms holding an ax. To my neck."

"What if you don't come back as you?" He rustled in the bag, still avoiding all eye contact.

"What exactly do you propose, Marsh?"

He pulled out a shiny silver blade and shears. I sat, my mouth agape.

"I think we need to start with this." He stalked toward me.

I vomited on his shoes.

CHAPTER 6

I couldn't even muster up a fake apology. For the first time in my pregnancy, my nausea wasn't an irritant. Acidic bile filled the room, and I had never been prouder. If I could learn to puke on command, I could probably rule the world. Or at least have people leave me alone.

"Annalise, it's okay. Don't worry," Marshall said. He kicked his shoes off and poured most of the remaining water from the pitcher on my tray over them. "This morning sickness is really bad. I forgot to bring you something for it."

"Are you kidding me?" I asked.

"Of course not. I'm the cook, I've helped a few other women with it before. I—"

"Not that. The blade. What the hell is that for? Are you going to amputate my leg? Or disfigure my face? Because I vote no on both."

"No." He sounded incredulous. "Of course not, Annalise. It's for your hair. We need to cut it off. All of it."

"Okay, how is that going to keep me alive?" I crossed my arms, still sitting on my cot. "Ridding my hair of rat's nests isn't the lifesaver I was thinking of."

"The only way to keep you here while you recover is to have you hide in plain sight. I figure that if we can disguise you as a man, you'll still be a scrawn, but you can work. You won't be restricted like the women."

"I'm not a lumberjack. I've been around it, I've seen it, but I don't know if I can keep up with the other jacks."

Marshall touched my knee. "You have to do your best."

"What if they want to make me a mechanical?"

"We'll have to cross that bridge when we get there. Besides, I don't think they let scrawn become mechanicals anyway."

"I don't know."

"Think about it, if something were to really go bad, no one is going to question a lumberjack wandering off into the timber. Not for a few hours, at least. I don't see another way. And no one will recognize you once we put you in baggy clothes and you're bald. We can prepare everything for our escape."

"Bald." It was neither a question nor a statement. The word tasted sour on my tongue. Maybe it was the lingering barf, but still, it felt wrong. "I don't want to be bald." I stroked my long hair then sucked in a deep breath. "But I also don't want to be dead."

"That's the spirit." Marshall beamed.

"Okay." I clamped my eyes shut. "No time like the present. Chop away."

"Are you ready?" He reached into the bag and pulled out a worn piece of parchment. "Because if you want to think about it, there are other things we can go over instead."

"It's only hair." I grabbed the scissors and cut a section short, right up to my forehead.

Marshall gently regained the scissors from my death grip and finished the job. My beautiful hair fell in golden piles around me. I touched a silky lock and rubbed it between my fingers. A tear worked its way down my pale cheek. Why was I being such a baby? I said it myself—it was only hair.

Hair that I was losing because of Lumberchief Paul. Hadn't he taken enough? He stole our right to live, have families, our freedom, and now I was losing myself.

I reached up to instinctively push hair behind my ears, but my fingertips were empty and instead felt short stubble. A swishing noise grabbed my attention. Marshall lathered soap in a mug with a thick brush. This guy wasn't messing around.

"I'm sorry." He stood behind me. "Tell me what happened in the timber."

"What's to tell?" My voice hitched just for a moment. I wasn't sure if Marshall noticed; I hoped he didn't.

He methodically applied the foam in circular motions. "How did you outmaneuver the mechanicals? What was it like out there in the timber, alone at night?"

"It was cold. And damp." I heard the razor chopping down the little hairs on his first pass.

"Be still." He rested a hand on my shoulder. "Tell me more."

"Well . . ." I continued. I recounted the chase in detail, how the incompetent mechanicals were mere feet from me but were more intent on destroying than actually finding me. "Oh, and I saw a keringer."

He jerked his hand back. "What?"

"Yep . . . well I should say I *saw* and *felt* one. It ran right past me, brushed up against my arm."

"Annalise, I can't believe it. How did you get away?"

"Remember all that blood I lost?" The razor made another pass and another. He folded my ear over, careful not to cause any more injury to my already trauma-riddled body. "The keringer found my puddle of blood where I had been lying, and while he was feasting on that, I took off. Thankfully, the eyes on those monstrosities are mostly useless or I would have been done. You should have seen his wings, Marsh. They were huge. As big as this tent!"

"Maybe that stick in your leg was actually a good thing." He wiped my head with a towel that he'd pulled from his bag of tricks. "All done. We'll need to do this about once a week."

I grazed my fingertips across my scalp. The surface felt foreign against my hands. "Hopefully, I'll get out of here sooner rather than later. I'd like to let my hair grow before I pop this kid out. I don't want to be balder than my baby."

"Your baby," Marshall whispered. "Here." He handed me the piece of paper he had pulled out before. "I mapped out the distance today after breakfast. It looks like the most direct route to Crempshaw Camp is an old road. It was called the Gibson Trail in its heyday, although it seems to have been abandoned. Anyway, it's 127 miles."

"Damn," I said. I rested a hand on my smooth head.

"Yeah, it's far. I'm sorry, Annalise."

"Stop apologizing, Marsh. Just give me a minute and I'll come up with something."

He opened his bag once more. "I need to clean your leg and change the bandage. Then, I have to get back. Provisions will be here soon." Easing me onto my back, he straightened my leg and cleaned away the now dried blood. A bouquet of sap and essential oils replaced the vomit scent lingering in the air. Stinging sensations worked their way up my leg and into my thigh. I breathed deeply, staring at the moldy ceiling of the tent.

"What if we take a wagon?" I blurted out.

Marshall paused. "Are you suggesting we steal one from camp?"

"Unless you happen to have an extra wagon lying around your kitchen, then yes. That's exactly what I am suggesting."

He pressed the tender skin around my scab. "No signs of infection. That's good. The oils seem to be working. You'll be able to walk freely and integrate with the others in a day or two. You'll still be sore, but as you said, time isn't on your side."

"Marsh." I pushed his hand away. "I don't see any other way. How many other women are pregnant? Even if they weren't, that's too far to walk. Some of those women are eight months in. They need a mode of transportation. If we take one of the steam-engine wagons, we can get there in four, maybe five days. They're pretty big. I'll bet it can hold at least fifteen people, maybe even twenty."

"We'll need supplies," he said. "Food, water, wood, and weapons, in case we encounter a keringer or Paul comes after us."

"That's where you come in. I think I'll be able to scout out a wagon no matter what work they assign to me. I should be able to score wood too. Can you hoard some extra food for this?"

"Yes. I'll just rearrange rations over the next few days, maybe a week tops."

"A week?" I asked. "Some of these women might not have a week before they go into labor."

"This isn't going to happen overnight, and you saw firsthand what happens without a plan. We must do this right. I can only ration the food so much. I'll need to make some flatbreads, dry some meats, and gather water."

I lay back and rested my hands over my burgeoning belly. "You're right. Again," I mumbled.

"But the real test lies with you. Can you pretend to be a man and avoid Lumberchief Paul for that long?"

"Yes." I gave a single nod. "I basically spent my entire childhood avoiding him. It's not like we were ever close, so I have no burning desire to reunite with him. I just have one question."

"Shoot."

"What's my guy name going to be?"

CHAPTER 7

"How about Luap?" I asked.

"Luap?" Marshall looked at me sideways.

"Yeah, it's Paul spelled backward. And I'm the exact opposite of him, so I think it's fitting."

"I think that's, um, great. Sure."

I pushed myself up and off the cot and rolled my eyes. "I'm kidding, Marsh. This is actually kind of perfect. I can try out a name, and if I like it, that's what I'll name the baby."

"That's a lot of pressure."

"Not really," I said. "It's more pressure if I have to name this kid cold turkey. What if I hate the name after a few weeks? I don't want to give him an identity crisis." Not like the one I was currently having.

"You might have a girl," he said.

"I'm not that lucky." I leaned on a rusted cistern. "Angus."

"Angus?"

"Yep, Angus Nathaniel Rodgers." I lowered my voice an octave. "Just call me Angus. Or Ang. Or Gus. Actually, call me Angus."

"Marshall," a voice called from outside the tent.

I cursed and hid behind the cistern and pulled a sheet of dusty canvas over the top of myself. I peeked around the edge and saw a large lumberjack burst through the tent flap.

"Dare you is," he said.

"Yep," Marshall said. "Right here. That's me."

"Whudder you doin' in da supply tent?" He hiccoughed.

Ugh, drunk already? It couldn't have been later than ten or eleven in the morning.

"Getting supplies." Marshall's posture slumped and he turned in my direction.

"Wer lookin' for ya."

The lumberjack was at least seven feet tall and half as wide. He wore a tartan plaid shirt with thick blue suspenders attached to his dungarees. He turned slightly, and I caught a glimpse of a hatchet instead of a hand. A mechanical.

"I see that."

"Was dat on yer apron?"

"What?" Marshall's head flopped forward.

"Is, is dat hair? You got some gurl in here wit you?" He whistled. "Oh boy, guys come getta look at dis." Luckily, no one came when he called.

"No, no," Marshall said. "Of course not. I must have gotten it while I was cleaning up."

"You bedder not have a gurl in here. You're notta breeder."

"Didn't you say you needed something?" Marshall said, changing the subject.

"We's hungry." He rubbed his potbelly.

I leaned back and rolled my eyes. This guy was an idiot, but he had the power to get us both killed if we were found out.

A discarded silver water pitcher lay on its side, just out of reach. It must have gotten missed when Paul sold off or traded all things he deemed frivolous. I knew I was bald, but I hadn't *seen* myself bald. This was my chance, and it provided a good distraction while Marshall dealt with the jack. My heart rate quickened. I slowly slid my hand out of my hiding spot, grasped the cool handle, and yanked it back.

I spat on the widest part of it and wiped the dust away with my sleeve. It was still a little tarnished, but let's face it, so was I. Marshall said something back to the jacks, but I barely heard them. I lifted it to eye level.

Ugly.

Angry.

Distorted.

Possibly deranged.

I looked more like Paul now than I had with hair.

The reflection didn't belong to me. I sucked in a sharp breath, dropped the pitcher, and pushed myself back, accidently kicking over an oil lantern.

"Da heck was dat? You do gotta girl back dare, dontcha?"

Crap. I stilled, doing my best to be as silent as possible. Sweat broke out over my brow.

"It's nothing," Marshall said. "Probably just a raccoon. That's why, uh, why I was in here. I was grabbing a few things and setting a trap for vermin. You know, to feed to the scrawn. Back to what you were saying—you needed a snack? Did Lumberchief Paul approve the extra rations?"

"Yep, show did. We been werkin on a big un out dare. We call her Punkin. She finally felled today." He walked toward the cistern with big, heavy, lumbering steps. "Dat oil lamp is leakin' everywhere. You're gun burn dis whole place down."

"Right." Marshall stepped in front of him, hands raised. "I'll clean it up."

"That's right you will, scrawn."

"Of, of course, I will."

Marshall bowed down to the lumberjack too easily for my liking.

"Why don't you go find a comfy seat and I'll be right in to make you something to eat, okay?"

Apparently, that satisfied the jack because he walked out without saying a word. Marshall rushed over to me. "Anna, what happened?"

"Nothing, I must have slipped."

"Slipped? On what?"

"I dunno? The ground? This place is a dump, it's hard to say."

I watched as his eyes lingered on the broken glass. "We can't keep you here much longer."

I cupped the back of my neck. "I know."

"I have to go. As you heard, they knocked down 'a big un,' and I have to make them something to eat. Practice walking without a limp. I think we need to have you join the group as an outsider as soon as tomorrow."

My heart pounded hard in my chest. "Sure, no problem. You better get out of here. Didn't you say you had food being delivered today?"

"Anna." He squatted, tipped my chin up, and softly touched my head. "It'll grow back."

I pushed his hands away and stood. "Duh, of course it will. It's hair, not an arm. I'm fine. I just slipped. And look . . ." I ran as best as I could in the small area, wearing the mask of a happy person. "I'll be better tomorrow. You better get out of here before he comes back."

"Sure." Marshall's lopsided grin wasn't fooling me, but it was better this way. I studied his face for a moment longer. His wide nose and full lips fit his face perfectly. His face was strong, like him. The *real* him, not the timid person the Scrawn Law forced him to be. He pushed the bag toward me once more. "There are some clothes and boots in there. I hope they fit. If we're lucky, you'll blend in with the other lumberjacks."

"Yeah," I said. "Lucky."

When I was certain he was out of earshot, I calmly picked up the towel he had used to wipe my head. I sat on the cot. My leg throbbed, but my heart hurt worse. I buried my face in the coarse fabric and allowed myself to cry until I fell asleep.

CHAPTER 8

I peered in the bag and pulled out heavy, sticky clothing. Clearly, Marshall didn't bother getting me clean clothes, which surprised me. Even though his clothes were hand-me-downs, he always managed to look polished. No matter how threadbare, his pants were always pressed with a perfect crease, and his shirt was free of blemishes and tucked in.

Stains of sap and mud made me more authentic, I guessed. Thick, tan canvas pants rested on the bed as I took inventory of the rest of the clothes. Red base layers were a happy sight, and I welcomed their warmth. The ragged nightgown I'd escaped in wasn't exactly built for cold weather. Before I tugged on the long underwear, I changed into a fresh bra. It was too small, and would be great at smashing things down, but my tender breasts felt like an anvil was pressing onto them. My big toe caught in a small hole on the left knee of the pants as I stepped in. I tucked in my oversized, wool, navy-blue shirt and slipped a woven pair of olive-green suspenders over my shoulders. They held up my pants nicely. Lastly, I pulled on the heavy boots; tucking my pants into them, I laced one, then knotted the other since the lace was broken.

I grabbed the black leather gloves and green beanie and stalked around the tent. A cracked mirror was propped along one of the walls. With the warm beanie now resting on my bald head, I gave myself a once over. From head to toe, I was a bona fide lumberjack. I wasn't sure if I should have laughed or cried. The reflection revealed a missing button on my cuff, so I rolled up both sleeves just below my elbow. Red long johns peeked out on my forearms. Bits of anthracite were scattered on the ground. I rubbed a piece of coal between my hands and smeared some on my forehead and cheeks.

"Looking good, Anna."

I gasped. "Dang it, Marsh. Are you trying to give me a stroke?" I whipped around, slowing my breathing. "And it's Angus."

"Right." He held a tray. "Angus."

"Honestly, what do you think?" I asked. Arms splayed out, I did a quick turn.

"You look like a lumberjack. I'm glad the clothes fit. But don't do that again; guys don't spin."

"Tell that to the girls. My boobs are completely squished. And the boots are a bit big, but I think if I can snag another pair of wool socks, they'll fit."

"Good. Come." He pointed at the cot. "Sit, eat, we need to finalize your arrival at camp."

The boots still felt heavy and foreign, but I did my best to walk normally, with nothing more than a slight limp. No way they'd accept me into the camp if I was outwardly injured. It still hurt, but I was good at ignoring things. I sat and took in my surroundings once more. This was the last time I'd be this safe for a while. Not that I was truly safe, but I could pretend.

The food tray held pot roast in a thick, brown gravy atop mashed potatoes. I greedily lapped up my dinner. Out of the corner of my eye, I noticed Marshall taking off his shoes.

"Marsh," I said with a mouth full of starchy potatoes. "Come on, I'm trying to eat." I shoved another spoonful in my mouth. The plate was empty within a few minutes, and I used a small piece of stale bread to sop up the salty gravy.

"Here." Marshall stood barefoot on the cold ground. "Take them."

"Your socks? I can't take your socks."

"You can and will." He tossed them at me.

"It's kinda gross to wear your old socks," I mumbled.

"Annalise—"

"Angus."

"*Angus*, do you know how hard it was to steal an entire outfit? I can't promise when I'll be able to lift another pair of socks. I can do without for a while. But if you're stumbling around in your shoes, it'll draw more unneeded attention directly at you. You've already got your leg to deal with. Let's not add to the problem."

Without meaning to, Marshall had pointed out that I was, in fact, a problem.

First, I hobbled back into camp and put my friend in a terrible position where he was forced to hide me and bring me food. Then, I complicated things by making him take care of a nasty wound; I'm sure that was just a blast. Next, I made him to steal a bunch of clothes at the risk of having his hands cut off if he would have gotten caught. And the finale? I took socks right from his feet. I felt lower than a pile of sludge. In the last few days, I'd become the most self-centered person at Younish.

Besides Paul. And he was a monster.

"Well, I guess I'll make do with these," I responded coolly. "So, I've done some thinking, because that's literally all I can do from here."

"Good. What's the plan, Anna—Gus."

"I'll slip out the back. I don't think that'll be a big deal. I mean, it's not like the jacks are prisoners here, not like the women and scrawn. I'll just waltz right out, run into the timber, double back, and make my way toward the entrance." By now, I was pacing and talking with big hand gestures. "Then if anyone asks, I'll say that I want to join Younish because I had to leave my old camp since my older brother is a complete wacko and giant piece of sh—."

"Come on, Annalise." Marshall rested his hand on my shoulder and faced me. His dark eyes bore holes into me. "You have to be serious. And you need to practice calling yourself Angus."

"Fine," I said. "I'll introduce myself as Angus Nathaniel Rodgers and say I want to join the camp. Satisfied?"

He rubbed his hand over his tight curls, then over his face. "When will you feel up to it?"

"Tonight. No reason to wait until tomorrow. Plus, exactly zero percent of them will be sober, so it'll be easier to convince them to take me in. Sound good?"

"Yes. Good luck, Annalise."

"Angus."

I turned and walked out before he could stop me.

CHAPTER 9

Sneaking out was much easier on two feet than crawling with a useless leg after major blood loss. While my calf still ached, it was bearable. Whatever concoction of sap, oils, and leaves Marshall used, it had done the trick. Maybe he'd missed his calling as a doctor.

The camp wasn't originally built to keep people in, per se, but more to keep beasts out. Namely the keringer. Plus, the bigger you could make your camp, the better you looked to the outside world. Of course, that had all changed now that Paul needed the worthless scrawn to do the cooking, cleaning, and other undesirable jobs at the low, low rate of free ninety-nine.

Initially, I started out by hiding behind tents while trying to make my way out. I quickly realized this was probably a great way to draw attention to myself, so I abandoned the idea. Instead, I kept my head down and walked at a steady pace toward the back in search of a gap. It didn't take long to find one I could squeeze through undetected.

Once through, I made a mad dash deep enough into the timber that only the fire from the camp could be seen. My leg protested and I absently rubbed it, trying to quiet the angry nerves. With proper clothing this time around, the evening air didn't seem quite as cold. Aside from my foggy breath, I wouldn't have noticed the chill.

I made my way as close to the entrance as I could without being seen. I'd never been through the gates on my own. Aside from my escape, I couldn't remember the last time I'd left camp. The entry point itself was large, at least twenty feet across, and the wood spires jutted up into the air twice as high. It was the tallest camp and made for quite a statement.

Crouching behind a tree, I watched people filter in and out with ease. This was going to be a piece of cake. I'd just blend in, act like I belonged, then introduce myself in the morning when it was time to work. I stood, still watching carefully as I made my way out of the timber. As I got closer, a brick sunk deep into my growing belly.

People were not filtering in and out willy-nilly as I'd thought. Some were being stopped, and it looked like being questioned. I tripped over a tree stump and landed on all fours. Panicked, I scrambled and crab walked until I was behind a tree large enough to conceal me.

Crap, crap, crap. What are they doing? Why are they stopping some and not others? I had to get my nerves under control, but my heightened emotional state made it practically impossible. I needed them to believe I was a man. No. Not just a man, a lumberjack. A jack capable of working along the others, even if I was a scrawn.

I stood, brushed myself off, and took inventory of everything. My shirt was tucked in and pulled out enough to conceal my chest. It didn't matter if it caught on my belly. I was still small, and they would have thought it was a beer gut anyway. Shifting from foot to foot, I checked my pants, suspenders, and hat. I pulled the leather gloves from my pocket and wrung them like a chicken's neck. It helped calm my nerves. But no need to wear work gloves now, so I stuffed them in my back pocket.

I cleared my throat, used my best deep voice, and said aloud, "Hi, the name is Angus Nathaniel Rodgers. I'm Angus Nathaniel Rodgers. Name's Angus. Angus Nathaniel Rodgers, how the hell are you?" I hoped I could just walk by without giving a name.

As I got closer, I slowed my pace and watched two men go in. The first eased by with a nod, but the second was stopped. I strained my ears to catch the conversation without looking obvious.

"Name?" a guard said. He was over eight feet tall and wore black canvas pants with a black shirt. Despite the cold, he still wore his sleeves rolled up and had an ax hanging from his belt. Across from him, a mechanical with a double-bit felling ax for a left arm stood, looming. I wasn't sure if he was his crony or just a spectator. The combination of the campfire behind them and the shadows made for a foreboding way to enter camp. This wasn't by accident. This had Paul written all over it.

The man stopped. "Jethro Stephan Smith."

"What's your business here?" The guard's voice was deeper than I'd anticipated.

"I'm here to barter. I hear you make mechanicals, and I think I have just the right stuff."

"Merchant hours are over for the day." He flicked his wrist and the mechanical walked over. "Come back tomorrow."

"Surely, you can make an exception," he said.

Crap, what was I going to do? Aside from wanting to join the camp, I didn't have a reason. I was already taking a chance with my small stature. They'd allowed scrawn who were originally part of the camp to stay, but were they accepting new scrawn men? Would a guard weed me out before I could even plead my case to the lumberchief?

"Wrong answer." The guard nodded to the mechanical.

The mechanical swiped his double-bit ax hand with deadly accuracy directly in front of the merchant's nose. Could have skinned it if he wanted to.

The salesman put his hands up in front of him and slowly backed up. "I wasn't, wasn't serious. Just a joke. Kidding."

"Out," the jack guard said.

"Please, at least let me stay within the camp. Just for the night. Don't leave me out in the timber. You know what's out there. I've come all this way."

"You may stay outside the entrance. The fire from within the walls should be enough to keep you safe. But if you step foot into our camp, you will be made an example."

"Of course." The man backed up more.

I walked at a snail's pace and watched men walk in and out with just a nod to the guard. They must have been familiar with each other. Until one wasn't.

"Name."

"Davious John McMurphy."

"What's your business here?" the guard repeated.

"I'd like to join Younish Camp. I've heard about the eugenics, and I want to be a part of it."

"Is that so?" The guard smirked.

"Yes." Davious puffed out his chest. "I'm ready to defect to Younish Camp. I believe in a better race, and I think I could contribute to it. I have experience and I'm strong."

"*If* we accept you, pay starts at six-fifty on days you work." The guard waved the mechanical over. "Room and board will be deducted from that. And don't expect a paycheck if you're not pulling your weight."

They measured and recorded his height, weight, and chest. This was bad. Really bad.

"Seven-foot-one, two hundred and seventy-seven pounds, fifty-six-inch chest. What's your age, Davious?"

"Twenty-two."

The guard's stoic face slowly turned into a smile that didn't quite reach his eyes. "Excellent, Lumberchief Paul will be pleased. Wait over here. There'll be an evening announcement, and you'll meet the lumberchief after. Welcome to Younish Camp."

Oh shit, what am I going to do? I can't hide in the timber, it's too dangerous. If I can't get back in, how will I save the women? I cursed myself for once again not being prepared. Marshall was right, I should have had a real plan. But this was *his* plan. Then it hit me. I stopped and crouched to the ground. I unlaced my boot, pulled up my pant leg, and ripped off my bandage. This was my only chance.

"You there," the guard yelled. "Get off the ground and present yourself."

I walked as quickly as I could. My hands shook. The smell of the campfire filled my lungs. I cleared my throat.

"Name?"

"Name's Angus Nathaniel Rodgers." I lifted my pant leg. "And I'm here because I've been attacked by a keringer and lived to tell the tale."

CHAPTER 10

Lumberjacks loved to hear tales. Tall or true. Didn't matter. So this seemed appropriate.

"A keringer?" The guard crouched to examine my leg. "You survived a keringer attack?"

I crossed my arms, raised an eyebrow, and forced my lips shut. I wasn't sure what would come out of my mouth, nor could I be certain my voice wouldn't crack. Silence was better. If I could just make it past the guard, maybe I could go undetected and fly under the radar until it was time to escape.

"Better get his info and let him in." He motioned to the mechanical, who wrote down my measurements as the guard called them out. "Lumberchief Paul will want to hear about this. Six-foot even—that's too bad. Two hundred and four pounds. Let's record your chest and shoulder measurement and we'll be done."

My heart raced; my cover would be blown in a matter of seconds if he started poking around my soft chest. "Uh, my chest? Why?" I cleared my throat. "Why would you need to bother with that?"

The mechanical tilted his head to the side and examined me. "Because Lumberchief Paul documents everyone who comes through these walls."

"But you already said six-foot was bad. So I guess

the rest doesn't matter, right?" I asked. "Let's just save you the time and let me get off my feet. My leg is really starting to ache. Just write me down for a forty-five-inch chest, okay?"

"Come on," the mechanical said. "Our shift is almost over, I'm hungry. Someone stole my nosebag at lunch and I'm not missing dinner."

I rolled my pant leg down and rubbed my achy leg.

"You got a story to tell, so that'll do. Never met anyone who has lived to tell about a keringer encounter." The guard sighed. He pointed to the direction where Davious was patiently waiting. "Park it over there until the evening announcement. Then you can tell your tale."

"Cool." I started toward Davious.

"Angus?"

My spine stiffened; I squeezed my eyes shut and let out a deep breath. "Yeah?"

"How old are you?"

Relief washed over me. "Oh that. Yeah, I'm nineteen."

"Good," the guard said. "You still have time to hit another growth spurt. Maybe you won't be a scrawn after all."

"Scrawn?" I feigned.

That same smile I'd seen before crept up on his face. "I'll let the lumberchief explain that one." He laughed.

I walked several hundred feet toward the main bonfire in the middle of camp. I nodded at Davious, but kept my mouth shut. His long blond hair peeked out the bottom of his beanie; his brown eyes made a nice contrast. He was handsome. *What am I doing? Focus, Annalise.*

I took in the crowd around me with fresh eyes. I'd always seen it through the perspective of a woman, and most recently a scrawn.

Men in tan, black, navy, and olive-green pants stood around leisurely after what I was sure was a long day in the timber and waited for a delicious dinner provided by the one and only Marshall. They all wore button-down, long-sleeved shirts similar to mine. Most were solid red, blue, black, brown, mustard, and green, but a few wore plaid. Many had their sleeves rolled up, exposing their long underwear. Thick forearms bulged. Pants were tucked into their boots.

The men walked around talking and laughing. They'd occasionally walk to a wooden barrel filled with what I assumed was ale or dehorn. Paul was proud of his moonshine. A scrawn refilled his small, hollowed-out wooden mug. It surprised me that the alcohol was unlimited to all men.

I'd seen a few of these mugs of ale from a distance, but never up close like this. It was fascinating. Each one was uniquely carved—some had faces etched into them, others had names or random designs, many left large pieces of rough bark on them. I wondered if they had carved their mugs themselves or if they'd bartered for them from traveling merchants. Handles were made of sheds from deer or elk antlers, and it seemed the bigger the handle, the higher the ranking. Were these mugs a sign of a hierarchy? No, they were too stupid to do something that clever, I concluded.

Someone played a happy tune on a banjo. This was a full-on potlatch. I knew they had gatherings every night, but I never knew there were parties. They all seemed so . . . content. Now I understood why the men, even the scrawn, stayed. They were clothed, fed, sheltered, and given a nightly rager.

It was unfair.

Nights were the worst for the women. Before the

Scrawn Law, women were confined to their sleeping quarters, but nothing was too policed. I had never bothered wandering out unless it was to steal some private time with my love, Walter. Now, we were confined to a single, dirty, dank tent. The heavily pregnant women got the sleeping pads; the rest of us were lucky if we found enough space on the hard ground to spread out. It wasn't much better for the non-scrawn women. Breeding women were kept nearby; all of them had cots, but they were guarded. Paul couldn't risk one of them getting pregnant without approval.

I watched as the crowd slowly parted and six men carried in *him*. On top of a platform was a throne. The gnarled and twisted wood exposed beautiful grain. Deep lines of weather showed the age of the old, petrified branches. Arms weaved in and out and flanked the sides. At the top, they formed claws. Perfect holders for his ornate mug. I was in awe. It was a beautiful symbol of hatred and greed.

I studied the cup; it was different than the others. Its handle was a keringer saber-fang polished to a high sheen. I was certain he'd swiped the fang from some unsuspecting dealer. He didn't earn things; he stole. That's just how Paul was.

The crowd grew silent. Davious, the new recruit, looked at me for guidance. I shrugged and ducked out of his view. The fire crackled loudly in the silence. Smoke curled high into the dark sky. All eyes were on Lumberchief Paul.

All I could focus on was my hatred for my dear brother.

CHAPTER 11

"Here ye, here ye," Paul said.

I rolled my eyes. *How were we from the same family?*

"The horizon has moved up." He raised what should have been his left hand. A grafted chainsaw, just below his elbow, remained. He usually removed the saw while in camp, and all that was left was the motor. "And now we celebrate the twilight." The men clapped and cheered. Paul pumped the engine arm in the air and downed the contents of his mug. "Another successful day at Younish Camp."

The embers of the fire drifted lazily into the air. The heat from the fire momentarily distracted me. Shadows danced across the greasy, sap-stained faces of jacks across from me.

"Once again, I ask for your patience." He paused to take another drink. "Why is this always empty?" He shoved it to a scrawn, who quickly dipped into the dehorn barrel and deposited it onto one of the throne's knotty hands. Paul snatched it by the handle and took a long pull. "The eugenics program is coming along nicely. I have exciting news. We're already speculating four successful pregnancies and expect more in the coming weeks. The work and sacrifice you are doing today will change the future for generations to come."

Men cheered.

"Already?" I accidently said aloud. I cringed. Those poor women, forced to sleep with whomever Paul saw fit.

A jack's lip parted into a smile. Pearly yellows hung from diseased gums. "Isn't it great? We'll have the beginnings of our super race in no time. It will mark the beginning of an era!"

"Yeah." My hand absently went to my belly. "Great."

Paul raised his hand to calm the celebration. "We will be releasing another baby and its mother in the coming days. The scrawn is showing early stages of labor." The crowd was mixed with cheers and grumblings. "Now, now." Paul drained his cup once again and handed it off for another refill. "I know some of you don't necessarily agree with the *policy*. After all, they were pregnant before the Scrawn Law was enacted."

"You mean before you murdered and stole the lumberchief position?" I mumbled under my breath.

"But"—he stood from his throne and onto the platform—"if I didn't enforce it, where would we draw the line? What would we do with the new scrawn babies? They must be released in order for us to have a genetically gifted society."

"What happened to the old lumberchief?" I yelled. Immediate regret washed over me, and I fell back deep into the crowd. I cursed myself. Sometimes, I just couldn't keep my big mouth shut. But I knew the truth. I knew Paul had done *something* to him. I just couldn't prove what that something was.

Paul took an uneasy step, trying to gain a better vantage point. "Who said that?" He stumbled back into his throne. "This will be the last time I address this." He took a long pull from his mug. "Walter had an accident. End of story." His speech was slurred.

Accident, my ass. I clenched my jaw.

He hiccoughed. "And lucky for you"—hiccough—"he was training me to be his successor." His head fell to his chest for a moment. "Where are my new recruits? Everyone else, leave. You're dismissed."

Successor? They were practically the same age. Bull. And yet, they all just accepted his answer.

He drunkenly stepped off the platform before the scrawn had a chance to fully lower it, and he nearly tripped. A hand grabbed my bicep and led me toward Paul. "You better beef these up if you want to stay. You have lady arms," the guard said.

I tensed. This was it. If he recognized me, I was done. The women were done. It was all for nothing. I balled my hands into tight fists and released them over and over. Sweat dotted my upper brow. My knees threatened to give out.

"Hello, Lumberchief Paul," Davious said. "I'm excited to join your camp. I have a lot to offer. I can lift—"

"Yes, yes." Paul waved him off with a lazy wrist. "You"—he turned toward me—"are the one who fought off a keringer?"

I stared at him blankly. I hadn't been this close to my dear brother in a year. He'd grown even more. Until we were sixteen, I was taller and stronger than him. People used to call him a runt, and weak. He'd withdrawn into himself, and his only friend was Walter. When he hit his massive growth spurt, no one was more surprised than him. It gave him confidence to be a complete jerk. I stopped talking to him after that. He never missed an opportunity to berate smaller people with viciousness I'd never seen from him. He'd shot up eighteen inches and was just starting to fill out. Now, his broad shoulders stretched the fabric on his red shirt. The sleeve had been torn free from his left shoulder. The chainsaw arm. Dirt filled some of the creases in his tan face.

"Uh, yeah." I tried to look away, but his icy-blue eyes, a mirror image of mine, refused to let me break contact.

"How?" He smiled. His lips were wet, and his hot breath reeked of alcohol. His long, black beard looked messy from a distance. But up close, I could finally see the pine needles woven throughout were placed there purposely. Like a warrior. "Tell me how you . . . wait, you look . . ." he said, tilting his head. "I know you. Don't I?"

"Nope." I shook my head back and forth. "Sorry, but no. I just got here. So the keringer, they don't see good, right? Well, it jabbed me in the leg with its saber-fang, and I was bleeding pretty bad."

"I know I know you," he interrupted.

"Guess I just have one of those faces. I get that all the time." I bent over and pulled up my pant leg. "Like I was saying, it gored me, and I panicked. I jumped into a tree. The, uh, the beast was, well, sniffing around and lapping up the blood I'd lost before I jumped." The lie was coming together relatively well. "And then, uh, I squeezed my leg and let the blood drip below me until there was a big enough puddle to distract it. Since it mostly sees by scent, I left my blood behind and hobbled away. I'm mostly better now." Talking in a lower tone for this long was harder than I had anticipated.

Paul stared at me with bloodshot, watery eyes, head still cocked to the side, and his eyelids heavy. How drunk was he? Had he heard a word I'd said?

"Oh, the name is Angus. Angus Nathaniel Rodgers."

"Angus?" This seemed to perk him up a bit. "Angus?" He laughed. "That's a dog name."

"Excuse me?" I puffed out my chest.

"I had a dog named Angus when I was a boy." He was in full hysterics at this point.

Oh crap! How did I forget about Angus? I couldn't believe I had named myself after our childhood dog. It died before I hit age five, but still, I had good memories of the old boy. No wonder I liked the name.

"Tell me," I said, changing the subject, "about the grafting program."

"How old are you?" Paul swayed from side to side.

"Nineteen," I said.

"Unless you're still growing, you won't be breeding or grafting. I won't allow scrawn to do either. We lost too many in the past when we tried to graft them. Too weak. Waste of materials."

"What qualifications are needed to become a breeder?" Davious asked.

"Great question." Paul waved to the men and they carried his throne over to us. "You have to be at least six-foot-five, two hundred and sixty pounds, a fifty-inch chest, and between the ages of twenty and thirty. Don't be sad, Angus . . ." He tapped my shoulder. Chills danced up my spine. I held my breath. "You defeated a keringer, so we'll consider keeping you around. You can still work at Younish even if you're a scrawn." He plopped into his chair and released a long breath. "Grafting doesn't happen until you've been here six months. It's an honor that you must request."

More like horror.

"And the stronger you are, the better and stronger tool you get." He held up the chainsaw motor.

"Sounds fantastic." Davious beamed. "And the women? I assume there are size restrictions?"

"Strict size restrictions. The women must be at least six-foot-one, a buck seventy-five, and forty-inch hips."

"And the smaller women?" My voice cracked at the end. I cleared my voice. "The scrawn, as you call them. What happens to them?"

"We don't allow new female scrawn into the camp." He tried to take another drink from his empty cup. "Only men scrawn. But the ones who remain from before the law will live out their lives here. They're lucky. They'll get to watch history unfold before their eyes."

I furrowed my brow. *Did he really believe that?*

"They, of course, earn their keep. They do all the cleaning in the camp, but none of the scrawn women do the cooking. A few of them are still a little salty about the breeding program. And you know what they say." He winked. "Never trust an angry person with your food."

Paul's head bobbed up and down; he was close to passing out. "Just one more thing." He held up an unsteady finger. "Do not fornicate without my explicit permission, or else."

"Or else what?" I couldn't help myself. The boasting of this great program, the promise of a release within a few days, and thinking he was doing us a favor had worn my nerves raw. My big mouth threatened to get me in trouble again. But at least I wasn't choking him, so I was showing *some* restraint.

"You'll see." He smiled.

CHAPTER 12

As the potlatch dwindled, I found myself alone with Davious and my nearly passed-out brother.

"Thank you again," Davious started, "for this opportunity. I will not disappoint."

Davious's cuteness had completely disappeared in my eyes. Ass kisser.

Paul lifted his head slightly. "You will start with the buckers. They'll expect your cuts on the felled trees to be exact. If you keep up the good work, you'll find yourself as a faller one day."

Davious bowed slightly and took a step back.

"Me too?" I asked.

"No." Paul laughed. "A scrawn as a bucker? No, that would be a waste." He slurred his words so much I was having a difficult time understanding his jargon. "You'll be a knot bumper."

"A knot bumper?" I nearly yelled. "That's for kids. I mean, at my old camp, I took off branches and knots of felled trees when I was twelve."

"Yes." He smiled. "It's not a noble job, but it's a job. And you should be happy we even allowed a scrawn like yourself. A little gratitude would go a long way, Angus. We don't put up with much attitude or insubordination in my camp."

"Yeah, thanks for the job," I said. "Sorry, I guess I'm just a little tired. Speaking of which, I should probably go to bed." I turned and walked toward the sleeping tent.

"How do you know where we sleep?" Davious asked. Paul perked up, and I cursed myself for being so careless.

"I don't," I said. I turned to face them. "I was just going in the direction I saw the others head earlier. Where do we go?"

"Back over there." Paul pointed. "Follow me."

He waved at the scrawn. They heaved the heavy throne up in the air, and we followed them to a large canvas tent. A stack of blankets sat piled outside the door. My old job was to wash those same woolen blankets and pass them out. I hated every second of it.

"You'll have to pick out your own bedding. We seem to have misplaced our scrawn in charge of that."

"Is she lost?" Davious asked.

"She ran." Paul sighed. "Sick in the brain, if you ask me. But don't worry, we'll get her back. Until then, you'll be responsible for cleaning up your bedding. Pick any empty cot."

Misplaced? Was he kidding? I'm an object? Irritated, I swiped a heavy, red wool blanket as I walked in. I'd had enough of him; I skipped wishing him a good night. Besides, he was drunk. I doubt he'd remember much of anything tomorrow.

Uneasiness washed over me as I walked into the dimly lit tent. I'd been in this tent dozens of times. Mid-morning, I'd gather all the heavy blankets, which was no easy task. Some of the men used their blankets like tissue, so I was careful when I touched them, or I'd risk touching who knew what bodily fluid. Then I had to hand wash the soiled ones, hang them to dry, and refold and place them on the end of each cot. It was a disgusting job, and

I was certain the men used to be much more careful and hygienic when they were responsible for themselves.

The bunk beds were stacked four high and lined two opposite sides. The only thing separating them were the large wooden poles running down the center of the enormous canvas tent.

I hopped into an empty bed and lay back. A few oil lamps still burned, but it didn't matter—I was emotionally exhausted. Not even the symphony of snoring, that was just starting its first verse, was loud enough to keep me up.

CHAPTER 13

I heaved into the filthy toilet, if that's what you could call a hole in the ground. Last night's dinner had decided to make an encore appearance. Acid burned my throat. My stomach was completely empty now, but I continued to dry heave. Just looking at the men's latrine was enough to summon the vomit gods.

My body was slick with a cold sweat that sent shivers down my spine. I grabbed a towel to wipe my face on my way out and stumbled into a brick house of a man.

"Are you sick?" He squinted at me. "What illness did you bring in?"

My mind raced. I knew disease was grounds for immediate banishment. "I'm fine. I'm good." If I looked as green as I felt, I knew he wasn't buying it. "Honestly, I'm not ill."

"No, no." He blocked my path. "We can't be spreading no crud around here. We'll have to tell the lumber-chief."

"Wait," I said. "It's not, no, I mean . . ." I adjusted my beanie. "I, um, I'm new here, as you know. And I just celebrated, yeah, celebrated a little too much last night. The divine punishment. Need I say more?"

He stared blankly.

"You know . . ." I nodded. "I am hung . . ." I sang the last word hoping he would catch on.

"Over," he finished.

"You got it." I smirked.

"You've got to be careful with that dehorn. It's stronger than it tastes. Found out the hard way myself."

"Yeah, I'll try to learn my lesson," I said. "Hopefully, tonight won't be a repeat." I was going to have to figure something out. I could only use this excuse one more time before they decided I was stricken with something contagious and booted me.

Or worse.

"Looks like you enjoy your beer." He patted my belly.

I paled and held back my bile. "Who doesn't?" I ran back to the toilet and retched once again.

"Come have some breakfast. Nothing like a greasy breakfast to soak up the alcohol," he said.

"Yeah, I'll meet you there," I said.

Outside, a barrel of water beckoned me, and I happily splashed my face with the cold liquid. *Get it together, Annalise.* The cool droplets settled in the crooks of my eyes. *Angus. Angus Nathaniel Rodgers does not get sick. He kicks ass. Now get yourself to breakfast before anyone else starts nosing around.*

The air outside the tent was cool and smelled of fresh pine. Dewy timber released the fresh scent every morning, like cleansing the day. As I approached the mess hall, the pine was replaced by cooking oil and freshly baked bread. Loud chatter helped distract me from my churning, angry stomach. Men sat on benches, overturned stumps, and broken chairs.

I walked down the buffet line. It had been pretty picked through, but there was still some left. I guess the early jack gets the biscuit. I picked up a crusty roll and slathered it with white gravy. As it settled on my plate, bits of sausage shone through. Normally, I loved Marshall's cooking, but my morning sickness had other opinions. I filled a metal mug with coffee and found a seat at an empty bench.

"Is that him?" I overheard. "Yeah, that's the one."

"Here we go," I muttered.

I kept my head down and rearranged the food on my plate. This was the last thing I wanted to deal with at the moment.

The weight shifted on the hard, wooden bench as four or five jacks sidled up next to me.

"You're the one," a lumberjack in an olive-green shirt said. "You fought off the keringer?"

I kept my head down toward my plate and only lifted my eyelids in their direction. "Yep." I shifted my eyes back down to the plate. "So, new camp, new rules. Anything I should know?" I said, changing the subject.

"No way," another said, ignoring my question. "How'd you do it?

"You know, the regular way." I took a small bite. "What's it like working in the timber here?"

"Fine, not bad," the first jack said. "Come on, let's hear it."

I dropped my fork loudly onto the ceramic plate. "Do you mind? I'm trying to get some grub in me before the big day of lumberjacking. Not sure if you got the memo, but this is a lumberjack camp, not gossip group."

"No." A jack in a deep blue shirt bellied up to the table. "I'd like to hear a story with my breakfast. And I'd expect someone who has been lucky enough to join our camp to fess up real quick."

I stared blankly into his brown eyes. "I. Was. Attacked. By. A. Keringer. I. Won. The. End. Happy?"

He palmed his fork like a shovel and shoved an entire biscuit into his mouth, gravy dripping down his chin. "No, that's not enough," he said with a full mouth. The creamy gravy created a paste within his mouth, and I nearly heaved. "Tell me"—he swallowed—"how a shrimp like you killed a keringer."

"Killed a keringer?" I leaned back. "Oh, let's see." I put my finger up to my chin, and my eyes shifted to the top left corner of their sockets. "You see, it was a dark and dreary night. My parents had been murdered by a band of keringer. They shredded them to pieces. All that was left was hair and a few strands of their clothes. One ran right at me." By now, an entire crowd had surrounded me. "I sidestepped it, then another set me in its sights. I did a back flip over that one. Once I regained my balance, I wrapped my legs around the third one's head, spun, and broke its neck." I heard a few gasps. The man across from me had stopped eating and stared at me with wide eyes. I picked up my fork and waved it wildly. "That's how I got the gash in my leg. My calf caught on its saber-fang."

"What about the other two? I bet they was spittin' mad when they saw you killed one of 'em."

"Right, so then . . ." I whispered, and they all leaned in. I looked at the back of the room and saw Marshall leaning against a table, shaking his head. I did my best not to smile. "The first one came running at me, full speed. I sidestepped again, stretched out my fingers, and gouged its eyes out." I stood on my seat and stepped onto the table. "Then, the final keringer bellowed at me, angry, with revenge in its eyes. Pink froth from a previous kill dripped from the corner of its black mouth. I rolled onto my side as it came at me, and I punched straight up as it passed." I crouched and, with a balled fist, punched from down by my knee up past my head. "I ripped its heart clean out, and shoved it right in its face, still beating, until he finally expired. And that"—I jumped to the ground and grimaced, my leg protesting—"is how I killed *three* keringer."

All eyes stared.

"Really?" the man asked.

"Nope, just kidding." I turned and walked toward Marshall. "Now leave me alone."

CHAPTER 14

I rushed past Marshall and nodded for him to follow me out. A row of wooden barrels butted up against the mess hall. A perfect hiding place for me to puke.

"That was quite the tale," Marshall said. "Nothing like drawing unneeded attention to yourself, Anna—Angus."

"What was I supposed to do?" I coughed and retched until I couldn't breathe. "They wanted a story, so I gave them one. My idiot brother was so drunk last night, I doubt he remembers. Either way, he bought it. If this new version gets back to him, he'll just assume it's gossip. I'm sure in a year's time, he'll be telling this story as his own."

A warm hand rested on my upper back as I stood hunched over. "Are you going to be okay?"

I sat down and leaned against the barrels. "I honestly don't think so. I don't know if I can do this. How will I work if I'm this sick?"

"Look how far you've come already." Marshall squatted, and those dark eyes held my gaze. "You've defied the odds already. You can't let a little"—he looked around wildly, probably searching for eavesdroppers—"morning sickness stop you now."

"A little?" I gestured toward the contents of my

breakfast. "You call that a little? I'm pretty sure I puked up a boot. And it's not morning sickness, it a *hangover*."

"Good cover," he said. "Well, I promised I'd get you something for that." He placed a small tin in my hand. "It's peppermint leaves. Stick one under your tongue when you feel sick. It should help."

"It won't work." I pulled my knees up to my chest. "I'm so weak from this, I can't do it." A frustrated tear trickled down my cheek.

"You have to do it."

"No," I protested. "I can't."

He grabbed my shoulders. "Stop it. You're in too deep to stop now. Think about the women." He broke eye contact. "I heard one of the women might go into labor in the next day or two."

"What?" I sighed. "Paul said something in reference to it last night, but I just assumed he was exaggerating to get the crowd riled up."

"It's up to you." He stood. "Quit, give up, and leave now. Or give these women and their babies a chance."

Guilt washed over me. I knew the stakes.

I opened the cool tin, its rusty hinges squeaking with age. I placed a small, spiky leaf under my tongue. My whole mouth tingled with its minty sensation. Within seconds, my tongue was numb and chills ran through my body. I breathed deeply, fighting the nausea. "I hope this works, Marsh."

CHAPTER 15

The jacks and mechanicals filtered out of the mess hall and made their way toward the entrance. Some adjusted their pants to accommodate their full stomachs; others picked at yellow teeth with splinters of pine wood.

"Fall in line," Marshall said.

"Yeah." I stood. "No problem."

"Angus . . ." He paused. "Keep your eye out for a wood mule."

"Is that the thing that transports the logs?" I asked. "I haven't really been in the timber before—not when they're working."

"It is. You've seen them before, haven't you? It's basically a long wooden deck with a big steam engine in the middle. It has railings on both the front and sides, but not the back. We need it." He held the tip of his chin thoughtfully. "That should help speed up our escape."

"It'll also be easy for Paul to find us." I walked toward the entrance and kept my voice low. "We're literally giving him a smoke signal to follow."

"That's true." Marshall followed me closely. "I'll figure out a way to reroute the exhaust through the bottom. That'll at least give us a chance. If we have a warmer day, the smoke will mostly dissipate before it gets too high, I think."

"Can you do that?"

"Have you seen my kitchen?" Marshall laughed. "I've had to get creative and repair things in ways you'd never expect. My equipment is older than us. If I can rig up my stove, I can probably move the exhaust."

"Probably," I said reluctantly. "I probably won't die. I probably won't get caught. Cool."

"Get to work," Marshall said. He clearly wasn't buying into my dramatics today.

Davious walked past me. He slowly turned over his shoulder and gave me a side glance. His glance morphed into an accusing glare. I cursed.

"Yeah, well your breakfast made me sick," I yelled at Marshall.

"I'm sorry?" He tilted his head to the side.

"Don't let it happen again." I leaned in and whispered, "I'm sorry, I think Davious is getting suspicious. I didn't know what else to do."

"Right." He nodded. "Won't happen again, Mr. Rodgers."

I turned on my heel and walked toward the group. Men around me chattered about the previous day's bounty and hoping to find another 'punkin'. But my focus was on a silent prayer that I repeated over and over. After a few minutes, I found myself in a smaller, rougher group of men.

"Well, we'll see how it goes," a large man with a ginger beard said. "Could be another false alarm."

"How what goes?" I asked.

"Tonight."

I raised my eyebrows.

"One of the scrawn might be in labor."

I swallowed a lump in my throat.

"Hopefully, she can hold off until we're back," he said.

* * *

I followed the jacks and scrawn for forty-five minutes deep into the timber. By my estimation, I'd hiked roughly two miles. The throbbing in my lower leg begged for a break, but there was no time. We passed several clear areas. Based on the dozens of graying, weathered stumps, I guessed they'd been harvested quite some time ago. Amazed at the sheer size of some of the trunks, I pondered how I was going to pull my weight. Small saplings worked their way in between the cleared ground, rejuvenating the timber for the next generation.

As we got deeper into the timber, I watched a smaller scrawn break away and run ahead. No one seemed to notice, or if they did, they didn't care. Maybe this was my chance. I couldn't stop thinking about the poor scrawn in labor, though. She and her baby didn't deserve to be released. If it was a false alarm, this could buy me enough time to find a wood mule, steal it, and get everyone out. All I needed was a day or two. Marshall was crazy if he thought I was going to wait a week.

I slowly wandered away from the group just to scope things out. Surely, there was a wood mule nearby. Then I just had to write down its location and come back for it tonight.

Easy.

"You!"

I froze mid-step, closed my eyes, and let out a deep breath. Maybe I wasn't the *you* that was being yelled at. At least I hoped I wasn't. The sound of footfalls crunching leaves became louder.

I slowly turned around. "Me?"

"You lost?" The man was the same man with a ginger-colored beard I'd seen before. He must have been the leader. "I don't recognize you. You must be one of my new recruits." He looked me up and down and pulled a weathered piece of parchment from his back pocket.

"That's right." I bent to tie my already tied shoelace. "I'm new. I, uh, just got lost in the scenery, I guess."

"Don't get used to it. We'll log it soon enough." He never bothered looking up and continued to examine his paper. "Davious or Angus?"

"Angus." I stood.

"Welcome. The name's Frank Janssen. Since you seem to love the scenery, let's make you a whistle punk."

He was older than most of the men, maybe in his mid-thirties. Deep lines around his eyes and forehead told the story of a man who'd had a hard life. His red hair was a bit lighter than his beard, but all of that was overshadowed by his sheer size and girth. He was fit, tall, and wide. The odd thing was, he wasn't a mechanical, and I wondered why.

"Uh, I think Paul, I mean, Lumberchief Paul already gave me a job. A knot bumper."

"Look at you." He waved his hand up and down. "You're small, like a woman. You could shimmy right up to the top of those hundred-footers and scout out the best trees."

I'd never climbed more than six or eight feet up a tree. Heights weren't my thing. In fact, it scared the crap out of me. Scaling to the top of a tree wasn't an option. How on earth was I going to get out of this?

"Yeah . . ." I walked toward the rest of the group, which was now staring at me. "The lumberchief seemed pretty adamant about me cutting off the branches of the felled trees."

"You seemed so eager to get ahead of the group," he said. "And you *love* the view. So, a whistle punk it is."

"I . . . uh . . ." I stuttered to find a response and broke out in a sweat.

"It's true," Davious spoke up. "I was there, and I was assigned the noble job of a bucker. I'm Davious McMurphy."

I rolled my eyes. While I was thankful for his rescue, it was obvious he only interrupted because he wanted to show off just how special he thought he was.

This seemed to delight the redheaded leader. "Yes." He took ahold of either side of Davious's wide shoulders. "And a fine bucker you will make. You'll cut up in no time. Think of yourself as a butcher of the logging world." He turned to face the crowd. "Come everyone, I'd like to get paid today. It's only a few hundred feet up ahead."

Davious waited for me at the end of the line. "Trying to get out of climbing, are you?" He removed his beanie and ran his finger through his long blond hair. It made me miss my own.

"No," I lied. "I just don't want to make the lumberchief angry. He was pretty serious about me cleaning the branches off felled trees."

"He was drunk as a skunk." Davious stuffed his hat back on his head. "I doubt he'd remember."

"You should be careful what you say about the lumberchief," I warned. This guy had balls.

"I saw you with the cook today," he said, changing the subject. "You seemed pretty deep in conversation."

"He made me sick." I kicked a rock. "His breakfast did. I just wanted to let him know. That's all."

"I heard you were hungover and puked all over the pisser."

"You're just everywhere, aren't you?" I asked. *What was this guy's deal?* His interest in me set alarm bells off in my head. "Maybe you should write my biography since you seem to know all about me."

His face contorted into a mask of confusion. "I helped you back there. You'd be up in a tree if it weren't for me."

"Who said I needed help?"

"Whatever." He hurried away.

Not wanting to draw more attention to myself, I jogged until I was firmly in the middle of the group. A high-pitched whistle rang out.

Everyone stopped.

CHAPTER 16

The group fell silent as the whistle punk gave out his call. A few of the men looked up and listened intently. The whistle was followed by a series of other whistles. A code? It must have been, because the jacks led us to a behemoth tree they'd started the day prior.

The timber was so dense, I gathered this was the easiest way to retrace their steps. Force some unfortunate scrawn to climb a tree, sit perched like a bird, and direct the rest of us where to go. I guess if he fell, no one would care. Scrawn were less valuable than a tree.

I was in awe of the whole process. When the weather was extremely cold, they'd log near the camp, and I'd hear them. Occasionally, I'd see the top of a tree topple over. That was the closest I'd been to it. For now, I'd wait. My job didn't start until a tree was felled.

While the fallers sawed away at the trunk, the rest of the jacks sang songs while someone strummed on the banjo.

> *"Timber, timber, out all day, and in our slumber, keep us warm, fat, and rich. Timber is our life's blood."*

That particular tune, out of many, was catchy, and

I caught myself singing along. There was a strange com-radery for such a dangerous situation.

The tree was at least eight feet wide. I wondered how long they'd been working on it. First, two jacks seesawed a long, serrated blade back and forth until they grew weary. Sweat dotted their brows and their tired muscles bulged. Then, a mechanical stepped in with his chainsaw arm. Sawdust filled the air; the whirl of the saw drowned out the singing. Next, a mechanical with axes for legs leaned back on his butt and started chopping on the right side of the trunk. On the left side, a mechanical with a sledgehammer grafted to his head pounded it into the wounded tree.

It felt so . . . barbaric.

Suddenly, they both stopped. An unnerving quiet fell over the men. An angry groan bellowed from the tree.

"Timber!" the whistle punk yelled from above.

The lumberjacks had won, and the tree admitted its demise. Cracks and pops ripped across the forest. As if in slow motion, the tree fell toward the earth. I watched it slowly break at the bottom, its branches and leaves pro-testing the defeat as they crashed into other trees on its way down. The forest shook when it landed on the cold, hard ground. Everyone cheered. It was a fantastic sight. Another whistle sounded, and the fallers left to find their next job.

"Let's get to work," Frank announced. "We need to get this tree transport ready. We promised it'd be in Kansas by the end of the month."

I was up. As a knot bumper, my job was to quickly remove the branches. That was all I knew, so I paused to observe my co-workers.

They had a curved knife, sharp as a keringer's fang,

and as long as my arm. I found mine in a pile of recently sharpened tools.

They formed a line, and we worked our way down, chopping wildly with saws, sharp axes, and hammers. It was organized chaos, and someone was bound to get maimed at this speed. Good thing we were only scrawn, I guess. I chopped at my branch; the handle of my blade stung my hand with each repetition. Once removed, I carefully stepped over it and moved onto the next one. Within ten minutes, we were done. Branches lined either side of the felled tree, like flowers for a funeral on either side of the coffin.

Davious and the rest of the buckers were moments behind. Some were mechanicals, but others weren't converted yet, although I'm sure they were just biding their time until they qualified for the disgusting grafting procedure. They chopped the tree into smaller logs between six and eight feet. The whole thing was fascinating to me. I wiped my brow with a dirty, sawdust-covered hand.

Once finished, Frank walked by as a scrawn measured each one and called out numbers. I assumed it was for payment or to report to Paul. Furiously writing on his pad of paper, Frank moved from log to log. Once the calculations were done, he waved to a man approaching on a wood mule from somewhere in the timber.

Finally, there was the prize.

I studied the machine. The deck, as Marshall had called it, was easily fifteen feet long and provided a large space for trees. The wheels were similar to ones I'd seen on wagons, but they were taller and maybe a bit thinner. The railings were on hinges, and currently, one side was down for easier loading. A large claw picked up logs and stacked them on the back like a plate of sausage links.

One false move and they'd all go rolling off, crushing people in their wake.

How was I going to steal a machine like that without them noticing? And how the heck was I going to drive it? This was arguably the most important piece of equipment on site. My mind raced, and something in my belly moved.

A hunger pang? No, this was different. My heart pounded the inside of my sternum.

My baby.

I felt my baby move for the first time. A strange happiness that I couldn't explain washed over me. It was quickly replaced by sadness when I thought of the woman in labor, and realized in that moment, there was nothing I could do to save her. This was all happening too fast. Marsh was right—this wasn't going to happen overnight.

"Timber!"

A loud snap and a cry broke my train of thought. It was followed by a sick thud. The sound of a body landing on the ground from a high distance.

Broken.

The whistle punk had fallen.

That could have been me.

CHAPTER 17

In an instant, I was shaken back into reality and stared at the chaos before me. The whistle punk in our crew slid down from his perch at a pace so quick, I thought he was falling. He sprinted over. "Whistle Punk John! It's John from the crew ahead of us."

"Calm down," Frank said. "Take a deep breath. What happened?"

"A branch," he said breathlessly. "A branch from a felled tree knocked him from his perch." He rested his hands on his knees and looked up. "I saw him drop from the top."

Frank waved toward us. "Fall in line. This is a rescue mission." He turned to the whistle punk. "Get up on your perch, alert the other crews, and meet us over by him. Which direction was he?"

The whistle punk pointed west and gave what I assumed were coordinates. The crew started toward the fallen whistle punk, but I hesitated. Maybe this was my chance. They were distracted. If I could just figure out how to drive the wood mule, I could take it back to camp. I could—

"New guy—Andy? Er, Angus. Let's go!" Frank yelled at me.

I ran, careful to avoid fallen branches and debris on

the way. My chest burned. White breath pumped out of me as I sprinted with my crew.

A grown man screamed—not a frightened scream, but one of anguish. As we approached, there was a small clearing from where the tree had fallen and taken others with it during its descent. A jack was tying a rope around another one.

Four jacks and two mechanicals formed a semicircle, their backs to us. A collective gasp from my crew made me stop short. I slowly made my way to the front and tried to make sense of what I was seeing. It looked like the ground had caved in or swallowed itself. The rugged circle was ten feet across. The hole was littered with horizontal pine trees, some intact, others broken and missing most needles. It was so heavily covered in trees, I couldn't tell how deep it was. Exposed roots rimmed the edges, and the dirt smelled wet, like after a hard rain.

"What's going on? Where's John?" I asked.

I took a step, but a hand caught my chest. "It can't be," Frank said. "We scouted out this area for weeks. It was clear of keringer pits." He shook his head. "Hurry, get that rope secure and tied off. If we work quickly, maybe we can get John."

"Wait, what?" I asked. "John fell in there?" I pointed to the hole.

"You're the expert," Davious said. "Didn't you say you were attacked by one and lived to tell? What do you suggest we do? Or maybe, it's coming back for you. It smells your blood."

"I, uh, that's ridiculous. He can't smell my blood *inside* me."

"He drew him out."

"It's after his blood."

"We're doomed." The growing crowd grumbled.

"Well . . ." Davious folded his arms.

I felt all eyes on me. "I, uh . . . seriously, Davious, what's your problem?"

"No," Frank interrupted. "He's right, what do you suggest we do? No one here has ever encountered a keringer and lived to tell about it."

"I didn't go into its pit. I mean, that's its home. Why would I walk into its home? I'd basically be delivering myself as a meal." I cringed.

"Angus is right."

I heard footfalls behind me. I recognized the voice. Paul.

"We're not wasting any lives to recover a scrawn, whistle punk or not." Paul used the cutting edge of the chainsaw on his left arm to scratch at the dirt. "It's new—this pit is only a few hours old. Why didn't my whistle punks see this from their perches? He got what he deserved. He put *all* our lives at risk."

"Where did he come from?" I whispered to a jack in blue next to me.

"The lumberchief is always nearby," he whispered back. "Musta heard the commotion."

"With all due respect, Lumberchief"—Frank took a step toward him—"he might just be knocked out. He's a scrawn, but he's also a jack. We never leave a man behind."

"I said no." Paul's voice was fortified with anger. "Are you stupid? No wonder you never became a mechanical."

"I *chose* not to," he mumbled.

Paul turned toward the group. "Are you all trying to get yourselves killed? Move out. We must clear the area immediately. Bring all equipment back to camp. You'll be responsible for your own tools. We'll scout a new area tomorrow."

The jacks and mechanicals dispersed back to their collective crews. I picked up my curved knife and rushed toward the mule. "I can help with that," I offered.

The jack didn't reply.

The mule chugged to life and he drove off. My one chance to see how he operated it was gone in an instant.

My mind was reeling. What was I going to do? I didn't fit in, Davious was all over my business, and then there was the real threat of a woman in labor. I sucked in a deep breath. The cool autumn air cleared my senses. Jacks and mechanicals ran past me, away from the pit. I propped my heavy ax on my shoulder, trying to keep up, but I was lost in my thoughts. It wasn't long before we were halfway back to camp. No one wanted to hang out and wait for the keringer. Poor John.

We crested a small hill and saw several figures pulling green wagons behind them.

"Marshall, my good man." Frank rested a heavy hand on Marshall's shoulder. Marshall glanced at the filthy hand. I knew he'd be annoyed Frank was getting grease on his shirt. "No nosebag show today. We'll be eating our lunch back at camp."

"Cooks!" Marshall yelled. "Let's head back. They'll take their nosebags in the mess hall."

Five men, all with green wagons filled to the brim with silver lunch pails, carefully turned around.

Marshall furrowed his brow. "What's going on? Why are you headed back to camp?"

"There was an accident," Frank said. They walked step in step together. "We lost a scrawn today."

"What?" I could hear the panic in Marshall's voice. "Who?"

I wanted to run up to him and tell him I was okay, but Davious had already grown suspicious of our friendship.

The last thing I wanted to do was draw more attention to myself. Waiting to find him back at camp was the only option.

"I haven't even told you the worst of it," Frank started. "There's a fresh keringer pit out there."

"Wait." Marshall stopped walking. I took the opportunity to speed up my pace. If I hurried, I could pass him, and he'd see I was fine. "I'm confused. There was an accident? Was the accident a keringer attack?"

"The poor soul. It was a great fall," Frank said.

I was so close but couldn't walk any faster without drawing attention. Sweat dripped down my temple.

"The scrawn had the worst luck of anyone in the timber. He landed in the pit. And if the fall didn't kill him, the keringer certainly will."

Now was my chance. I brushed past Marshall, hitting his shoulder with my own. I looked over my shoulder, and my eyes locked with him. "Sorry."

Immediate relief colored his face. "No, no problem." He turned to Frank. "I'm sorry to hear that. I'll get these nosebags back to camp, and we'll set up lunch." The squeaky wheels of the wagon drew near. "Angus," he muttered. "I'm so glad. I mean, I'm sorry for whomever died. But I, I thought . . ."

"Not now." I stared forward, completely ignoring his presence. "Davious is suspicious of me. He's practically stalking my every move. Just walk near me and don't make eye contact."

Marshall passed me just enough that I could see his eyes drift down, to the left, and back at me. "I was afraid that might happen. Did you see any extra wood mules we could take?"

The red, gold, and orange leaves were a beautiful contrast against the bright blue sky and dark green pine.

The morning fog had burned off, and the afternoon sun brought a slight warmth. I stared a moment longer, delaying my response in case Davious was watching. "There *is* no extra equipment. I don't see how I can steal one without them noticing immediately. That'll completely blow our chances of getting a head start. Heck, we won't even have it long enough to load it with supplies without getting caught." Leaves crunched under my feet. "I don't know what to do, Marsh. Maybe this whole thing was a bad idea."

"I did some scouting of my own." I watched his smooth, dark skin pull tight across his face as he clenched his jaw. "I found an extra one, but it's not in great condition. It needs repair work, but I think we can fix it."

"Are you serious?" I responded too quickly. "Where?"

"It's on the north side of camp, on the outskirts."

I hadn't noticed it before, and I'd been out there just a few days ago. "It must be new," I said.

"I don't think so. Just go check it out before you go back into camp."

"Okay." I picked up my pace. "I'll meet you by the barrels behind the mess hall."

CHAPTER 18

I carefully made my way to the edge of a large group of men. Mainly watching for the back of Davious's blond hair. I was sure to stay behind him. The less he saw, the better. We were close to camp when I broke away. I wasn't as nimble as I'd been just a few weeks prior, but it was now or never. I doubled back behind a dense bunch of trees and brush. My face was moist with sweat, so I pulled off my hat. Jacks and mechanicals slowly made their way into camp.

It felt like I'd eaten my shirt. Cottonmouth was fierce. I tried to swallow, but it only made me cough. They were taking too long. I'd been crouching and my thighs burned. Enough of this. I stood. The cool air rushed over my bald head; it was a sensation that I didn't like. I slipped my hat back on.

"Hey, you," I heard someone yell.

I cursed. I was caught. As I started to step forward, I heard someone answer him.

"What?" The man walked toward him, and they continued their conversation. The first man, a shorter brunette, pointed his finger wildly. They'd lowered their voices, but he seemed angry. Or concerned. I couldn't quite tell. Were they talking about me? Maybe I'd been spotted and they were deciding how to deal with me before they busted my feeble hideout.

My breath quickened. I tried to come up with a reason why I was lurking in the trees, but nothing sounded believable. The taller man raised his hands up in defeat. The brown-haired man gestured with his hands and nodded. I surmised they were going to close the gates. This was an extremely rare occurrence. It happened last year during a howler. The old lumberchief was afraid the wind would rip through and destroy camp, so they closed the gates. But with the keringer looming nearby, I could understand why they'd close them.

Thinking of the old lumberchief brought back a lot of memories. Tears welled up in my eyes, but I pushed my feelings deep down, as I'd done in the past. Now wasn't the time.

I trekked through the thick brush. My leg throbbed. Once I was certain I was far enough around the curve of the camp, I left the cover of the timber.

There it was. A broken-down piece of junk lay before me like a dying beast. Grass had grown up and around the wood mule. Brittle pine needles and dead, rotting, brown leaves from several seasons were like carpet. My shoulders slumped. I walked to it tentatively. It leaned awkwardly from a broken wheel. Marshall had undersold its damage. I felt worse than before.

A puddle of sticky, black oil had pooled below the engine. Somehow, a small branch had lodged itself into the engine. I gripped the weathered twig; it broke apart in my hand. *Forget it. This is a lost cause.*

I was furious. Another failed plan. Failure-lise strikes again!

I stomped back toward camp, despite my injured leg. Then, I remembered the gate was most likely closed. I'd need to sneak back in. No matter, I'd done it before with a branch impaled in my calf. This would be easy as pie. Speaking of food, I was starving.

As I walked around the perimeter, looking for a gap, I lightly dragged my fingers across the bark on the spires. One by one, I felt the rough texture against my fingertips. My hand slipped through and I looked at the ground. Blood. More specifically, my blood. I bent and touched the dried puddles. Saliva gathered in the sides of my jaw; the familiar taste of bile crept its way up my throat.

I stood, rested my hands on my hips, and took several deep breaths of the cool autumn air. It curbed the nausea for the moment. No, I couldn't give up. I touched my leg. The memory of the baby being released and the woman's cries for help flooded back. Desperate screams burned into my brain. We could do this. I just didn't know how.

I reentered camp through the hole as if I'd never left. The mess hall wasn't too far away. I decided to come up from around the back so no one would notice me or try to direct me into the tent. Talking to Marshall was my number one priority. We needed a new plan.

CHAPTER 19

My stomach growled as I leaned against the hard, wooden barrel. Judging by the sky, it was probably two or three, and I hadn't eaten since breakfast. I hadn't exactly kept that down. I hoped Marshall would sneak me out a nose-bag. Exhaustion settled over me, so I sat between two barrels.

"Annalise?"

I rubbed the sleep from my eyes and cleared my throat.

"There you are," Marshall said.

"Sorry," I said. "I guess I fell asleep. And it's Angus."

"Here." He handed me a dented aluminum pail. "Lunch."

"Thank you." I opened the rusted lid. It squeaked in protest. Inside was a sandwich, some dried fruit, and a small glass jar full of soup. I greedily slurped it down and bit into my sandwich.

"Slow down." Marshall sat next to me. "Maybe chew up some peppermint real quick before you get sick."

I closed my eyes and chewed. "Good idea."

"What did you think? Of the wood mule."

"Is that a serious question?" I wiped my lips with the arm of my red long johns. "That thing is a piece of junk. We'll never get it fixed. The wheel is broken, possibly the entire axle. The wood deck is probably rotted out, but I couldn't tell because there was about four feet of pine needles and leaves covering it. And if that's not bad enough, the freaking engine was leaking and busted. What were you thinking? We have to find something else."

Marshall turned slightly and tentatively touched my shoulder. "Angus, calm down." His dark brown eyes grew wide. "You're shaking. It's not that bad."

"Not that bad?" I flicked his hand off me. "You're right. It's worse."

"Let me finish. I talked to the girls and—"

"You what? What did you say?" I asked.

"I told them we were going to escape, make a run for it. I only told the scrawn women. I wanted to feel them out, make sure it wasn't a lost cause."

"Marshall!" I stood. "They could have turned you in. You should have let me do it. You risked everything!"

"I had to. *We* have to."

"Do they know about me?"

"Not exactly."

"What does that mean?" I was growing impatient. Everything was falling apart, and I wasn't in control. I hated it.

"It means, I told them we had someone on the inside willing to help. I didn't tell them your name or that you were undercover. If I was going down, I was going down alone. I needed to give you and your baby a chance to escape."

It felt like someone had punched me in the gut. Marshall was risking everything for me, for the women, for the babies, and here I was yelling at him. Some friend I was.

"Marsh." I quickly hugged him. "You shouldn't have done that. This is my fault."

"Like I said, I had to. One of the women said her dad

is a mechanic. She used to work on engines and such with him before the Scrawn Law was enacted. I don't know the technical parts, but she said she'd fix it." He rubbed the back of his neck. "She said something about a rebuild. She got real technical . . ." He trailed off.

"Really?" I softened. "That's great."

"And I can fix the wheels."

"How?" I asked. I looked at him closely. His mustard-yellow shirt looked even more vibrant against his dark skin. Both his shirt and pants were perfectly pressed. But I could tell he was tired; this had been wearing on him. His apron was crooked, and his hair had grown out a little. I'd never seen him overdue for a haircut.

"I'll use two misery whips, bolt them end to end, wrap them around the circumference of the wheel, and cinch it tight."

"And that'll fix it?"

"More or less. I was also thinking I should take one of the extra canvas tents and strap it to the top for shelter."

"Oh yeah." I rubbed my chin. "Good call on that, Marsh. How long will this take?"

"We can work quickly, and I've already started rationing out extra food. I'd say . . ." He held his chin. ". . . Maybe five days."

"Five days," I said slowly, processing it in my head. "Okay, how can I help?"

"Anna." He stepped forward. He looked from side to side and held me by the shoulders. "Take care of yourself; you're going to have to work. Blend in, be careful, and when the time is right, we'll go talk to the remaining women together."

I nodded. "I can do that. I just hope the women can hold out that long. I heard someone might be in labor?"

Marshall's face darkened and he looked away. "Yes," he whispered.

He didn't have to say any more; it was written all over him. A woman and her baby would be released tonight. And there was nothing I could do to stop it.

CHAPTER 20

The walk to my tent felt foggy in my head. One of the scrawn was in labor and I had failed her. If only I'd figured out a quicker solution and gotten us out sooner. I wondered who it was? There was no telling. There were so many pregnant women. The terror she felt must have been unimaginable. The regret, fear, and anger were undoubtedly shared by the other scrawn women. It was like peering into a crystal ball of their doomed future. My future.

I'd botched the whole thing.

Stumbling toward the sleeping quarters, my mind was racing and my leg still burned. I was beyond tired. One step in and the wave of body odor combined with stale alcohol almost knocked me back on my feet. I'd need to find another place to rest.

I walked aimlessly around camp and found a large enough stump to rest on. Just as I got comfortable, a mechanical walked up to me.

"What do you think about the keringer pit we found?"

I didn't even look up. "Nothing."

"Well, do you think it's following us?" another asked.

"Maybe."

Lumberjacks and mechanicals alike kept coming to me for answers. I couldn't focus and gave them one-word answers. I tuned most of them out and resorted to shrugging.

I rested my elbows on my knees and thought back to when times were different at Younish. When I was a kid, I used to run around with the other girls. We'd laugh, sing, hold hands, and dance in a circle. We were raised by all the women; it was uncommon to have both parents alive. Lumberjacking was a dangerous job, and so was childbirth, for that matter. I'd lost both parents by the time I was six. But that was normal. I had lots of moms; they loved us all the same. We were all raised together. No scrawn, no breeders. Just one big family. Chores were shared by all the women while the men worked.

There was the occasional mechanical, but they weren't the norm. Grafting was only done when someone had lost a limb due to a logging accident. No one voluntarily grafted anything to a perfectly healthy appendage. Not like now.

Younish Camp of then and now weren't even on the same spectrum.

In just a few months, everything changed. It had become hell on earth.

The camp was overcrowded. Not to mention, the type of people it was currently attracting weren't exactly upstanding citizens. Quiet, peace, and happiness were all things of the past. I used to know everyone in camp; now it was mostly strangers. The original members were so few, and they rarely spoke. They were as beaten down as me. Losing our lumberchief had been devastating.

I stared straight down between my knees at the soft dirt, my cheeks resting on my palms. Moist tears wetted the earth. I missed him. Walter. He was one of the youngest lumberchiefs to lead a camp, only twenty when he took over four years ago. But he was smart, fair, and honest.

His father had mentored him well and led just like him, and the camp flourished. Morals and ethics were key. Unfortunately, he made the mistake of befriending my psychotic brother.

A squeaky wheel jerked me from my thoughts. I wiped my eyes with my sleeve and glanced up to see the commotion. My stomach dropped. A long wooden table, complete with stirrups and an elaborate pulley system, was being pushed into the center of camp. I watched as jacks carefully deposited the table right in front of Paul's wooden throne.

Surely, this set up would delight the sick leader. Front row seats to watch the scrawn's execution. He was playing god. Deciding who lived and who died, based on arbitrary, made-up reasons. I studied the setup a moment longer. Above the straps and stirrups was a long, black metal rod that held a pulley system. At the end of the rope was an iron-cast glove and ax.

I turned to leave as a crowd started to gather. I felt a hand on my shoulder.

"Oh yes," Paul said. "Here for the releasing, I see. You're in for a treat." I could hear him smile as he talked. I avoided eye contact, but I could see his breath in the air.

"Yeah," I replied. "I, uh, I'm not sure I have the stomach for it."

"How do you know? You've never seen one." He patted the top of my head like a dog and scanned the growing crowd. "Where's Davious?" he yelled. "I want my new recruits to see firsthand what happens when you decide to take the breeding law into your own hands."

Davious bounced over, happy to be recognized. Thankfully, it took the focus off me for a moment.

"I'm right here, sir," Davious said, chest puffed out.

"Excellent. It shouldn't be much longer. Stay right

here and enjoy." Paul walked toward a few jacks who'd motioned for him.

I glanced at Davious. "Are you seriously excited for this?"

"You're not?" he asked. "This is why I joined. For the super race. In less than fifty years, we'll have the strongest people on earth. If I'm lucky, I'll see my grandchildren grow up in a perfect race. And if not? I'm still a part of history." He crossed his arms, satisfied. "That's enough for me. I'll be a part of the first bloodline."

"And you're okay with what's about to happen here?"

Two scrawn helpers dragged a crimson-stained canvas cloth and placed it under the table. *To catch the blood*, I thought. It reeked of death.

Davious raised an eyebrow and looked at me sideways. "You're not? Why are you here?"

"I, just, I mean, of course, I believe in the super race," I stammered. "I don't think this"—I pointed to the table— "is right. It's a little extreme for me."

"Leave, then."

"Maybe I will." I turned and was immediately halted by the crowd that had formed. I took in the scene. Somehow, I missed the sun setting and the moon's arrival. The entire camp had shown up. But it was different. It wasn't like the potlatch from the night before. Everyone was here, men and women. The mood wasn't happy. Save for a few sickos like Davious, people weren't celebrating. Sure, there was plenty of dehorn, but ever since Paul took over, alcohol flowed all night, every night. Like I said, the people this camp attracted weren't exactly savory people.

"Welcome." Paul stood on his throne and raised his mug of ale high. "I do not take pleasure in tonight's releasing."

He couldn't fool me. I knew he loved this. Exerting his

power, showing his dominance, and above all, reminding everyone he held the key to their future.

"But," he continued, "it is necessary to remind you all what happens when you break the rules of the breeding program."

Cries of an exhausted and desperate woman echoed in the night. I turned my back to Paul and watched Jeanette, a scrawn I'd looked up to when I was a young girl, being hoisted onto the table. Her skin was slick with sweat, and her white nightgown clung to her.

"No," she cried out. She sounded so weak, her voice was nearly hoarse. "Please, no. I was with child before the Scrawn Law."

Two jacks strapped down her arms. Then they tied her legs to the stirrups, and her hand was forced into the iron fist.

"No!" she shrieked.

"Shhh." Paul held a finger to his lips. "And what, pray tell, are we supposed to do with this useless offspring? Where do we draw the line?" He took a long pull from his mug and carelessly rested it on the throne. "The rule has been set. And a camp without law and order is no camp at all. Dear Jeanette is a warning to anyone who thinks they are above the law. Proceed." He flicked his wrist, as if to initiate the final stages of labor. He sat and rested his cheek on his balled fist.

Jeanette's head thrashed from side to side. Her cries were desperate and strained. She looked as if she'd been without food or water for days. Pallid skin and cracked lips glowed in the moonlight. My hand instinctively rested on my belly. My baby. *His* baby. How was this happening?

I turned away.

A jack approached the throne, and Paul leaned down

to him. I watched as the man whispered into Paul's ear. A smile formed across his lips. He stood.

"It seems Jeanette is withholding her labor. Luckily, I have just the men to help."

I turned, and the horror deepened.

CHAPTER 21

Four men climbed onto the wooden table and stood and pushed on her swollen belly. *Were they trying to force the baby out? Did these idiots have any idea how babies were born?*

Jeanette's shrieks of pain and agony were deafening. I had to get out of there, but I was trapped. No, Jeanette was trapped. I was stuck. *Oh, Jeanette. I'm so sorry, I failed you.*

The crowd had grown silent as the men continued pushing and bearing down on her. Some of the women in the back, both breeder and scrawn, sobbed loudly. Paul stood again. "I will not have the drama from the crowd. If you must, look away and be quiet!"

Several hugged each other. But the comfort wasn't enough. They slowly slinked away from the crowd. No one stopped them. They were distracted. It was happening. The baby was ready to enter this cruel world. Jeanette's screams morphed into low moans. I prayed the baby would be stillborn. What a thing to pray for. But at this point, it would be the closest thing to mercy it would ever see.

The distinct sound of a newborn cry shattered my heart. I couldn't hold it together any longer. Tears rained down my face. I did my best to keep my breath even, but I was fearful of hyperventilating.

Jeanette's exhaustion took over. Her legs were released from the stirrups, and she lay flat, staring blankly at the sky. Her chest slowly rose and fell, the only indication she was still alive. My eyes darted to the iron fist her hand had been bolted into earlier. An ax, cast onto the fist, rested heavily on top. Who had created such a disgusting thing? A hand, holding an ax. Paul—only Paul's sick mind would create a monstrosity like that.

"No." Jeanette rolled her head slowly from side to side. "No," she mumbled, eyes closed.

Two jacks dressed in black canvas pants and matching shirts hoisted the ropes up, and the fist rose several feet in the air. Paul stepped from the throne to the table. He placed the shrieking baby next to its mother, its neck directly below the ax.

"Tonight, Jeanette Mulfino has paid the ultimate price. The sacrifice of both mother and offspring is her tribute to a new race. A better race!" Flames from the nearby fire danced on Paul's face as he spoke.

Several men cheered. My eyes darted to her arm. It was shaking; she was weak. She couldn't hold the heavy fist and ax much longer. She screamed a final time before her arm gave out. The weight of the ax welded to the metal glove came down swiftly. I looked away, but the sickening, wet thud was something I'd live with the rest of my life.

"The suckling has been released," Paul announced.

CHAPTER 22

The crowd erupted in mostly happy cheers.

I turned to run, but Davious grabbed me by my shoulders. He stared intently at me. I couldn't read his expression. "Not now," I growled at him. I wasn't sticking around to see Jeanette's releasing.

I ran as hard as I had the night I'd escaped. The last time a mother and baby were murdered. My lungs gulped in the cold air. Tears streamed down my face. I lost my footing and face-planted.

"Angus."

I rolled onto my back and stared at the stars. My chest heaved. Without warning, I started sobbing loudly.

"Angus, come on. Get up." A broad shoulder was firmly placed into my stomach, and then I was staring at the ground. I was being carried away. "Stop that, before someone hears you."

I couldn't control myself. Between the hormones and the horror, I didn't think I could go on. What was the point of this if I couldn't save Jeanette? What if someone else went into labor before we were ready? What if we were never ready?

I felt myself being placed on the ground. I opened my eyes, tears still flowing freely, and realized I was back in the supply tent.

"Angus," Marshall said. "Please, you have to stop. We're going to get caught." He sat me up.

"She," I hiccoughed. "The baby . . ." Fresh sobs erupted, and I buried my face in his shoulder. "The baby, Marshall, the baby!"

"I know." His voice cracked. "I know. But please, you have to be quiet."

I cried until I ran out of tears. I felt weak, drained.

"What are we going to do?" I asked.

"We're going to save the rest of them," he replied.

"We couldn't save Jeanette." I burst into tears. "Or her baby."

"Anna, uh, Angus. You have to calm down."

I counted my breaths in my head. *In, one, two, three, four, five. Out, one, two, three, four, five.* "Did anyone see me run away?"

"I don't think so. It was pretty chaotic when you left. I think some of the others are starting to have doubts—not just scrawn."

"Really?"

"Yeah." He looked over his shoulder toward the tent opening. "A few. Enough to cause grumblings." He put his shoulder under my armpit and tried to lift me. I relented and slowly stood.

"Marsh," I whispered. "Can we really save the rest?"

"Not if we get caught in here." He wiped my tears. "We have to get back. Paul made us prepare a late dinner, and they'll notice if I'm absent."

I walked to the entrance and stared at the ground.

"Angus!" He snapped his fingers in my face. "Wake up. You have to pretend you're on board with this while we're still here."

"Right." I nodded.

"After dinner, meet me at the breeders' tent."

"For what?"

"We're going to talk to the rest of the women. I'll bring the scrawn women. We need out of here as soon as possible."

"Okay," I said. "Sure."

He jogged toward the kitchen. I took a deep breath and hoped I'd be able to fake it the rest of the night.

CHAPTER 23

Dinner came, and I had no appetite. I spent my time rehearsing what I was going to say to the women. Finding a way to convince them to follow me and not turn me in was going to be tricky. But Marshall was right, this needed to happen tonight. Emotions were raw and we had run out of time.

Jeanette was dead.

I was staring down, aimlessly moving my fork around my plate, when a commotion started outside the tent. *What now?*

I walked out, expecting the worst, and squinted at the scene before me. A banjo started and someone tossed what I assumed was gas onto the fire. A whoosh of flames jumped into the night sky, and men laughed and cheered. A potlatch? Now?

I couldn't believe it. How were they celebrating at a time like this? Surveying the crowd, I realized there were two factions. One was partying and drinking the dehorn as if there was something to celebrate. The other were men drinking to forget. The former far outnumbered the latter, but it gave me hope there was some humanity left in the camp.

I felt someone staring at me and turned. Frank's eyes were locked on me. Was he mad? Upset? From what I could surmise, he was drunk, and definitely not happy. His watery eyes bore holes into me. They were a stark contrast from his fiery red hair and beard. A jack walked in front of me, blocking Frank's view, so I took the opportunity to fade into the crowd.

* * *

Once I was certain no one was following me, I made my way to the breeders' tent. Posted outside was a guard. Crap. How had we forgotten about them? Or maybe *we* hadn't. I suppose Marshall assumed I'd figure something out. I pulled my hat lower onto my head and puffed out my chest.

"I'm here," I said.

The man looked confused. "Huh?"

"I'm here," I said slowly. "For my shift."

Again, the brute stared at me blankly. "Your shift?"

"Yeah, what are you, deaf and dumb?"

Oops.

"What?" The man stood at least a head taller than me. He clenched his fists.

"I am here to take your shift. For the potlatch." I held my ground. "They said you deserved the night off. Wait, you didn't hear?"

"No, I didn't."

"Oh well." I turned on my heel. "I guess I'll get to enjoy the dehorn. I heard the ale is extra strong tonight." I felt a rough hand on my shoulder, and I smiled.

"Not so fast." He turned me around. "Tonight is my night to relax. You can watch over these ninnies. And watch 'em close. Lumberchief Paul says their chastity is sacred."

"Will do." I saluted him.

Once he was deep into the crowd, I pushed back the heavy canvas and stepped inside. The room was dark, save for a few lanterns, and smelled of burning oil and lavender. It must have been wash day. There were six girls in the room—one brushing her wet hair, another pulling hers into a long braid. All six froze and stared at me. Lillian, a friend I knew from before, sucked in a deep breath, as if to prepare for a scream. I knew her, but all she saw was a man standing in her tent.

I held up my hands. "No, no, it's okay. I'm here to help."

"What do you want?" Lillian stood stoically and protectively near the other women. "No one is scheduled to breed tonight."

"Lillian, it's okay," I said.

"How do you know my name?" Her voice cracked.

"Marshall told me," I lied. "I have a plan."

"We're not interested in your plan." She stepped forward. "Now kindly leave."

I felt a slight breeze and turned to see Marshall enter with the scrawn women.

"It's okay," Marshall said. "Hurry, everyone get in and close the flap."

The chilly evening air had snuck its way in; a few of the girls covered themselves in blankets. Marshall walked over to a small stove in the middle of the room. Its black smoke pipe snaked up through the top of the tent. He fed the hungry stove with leftover bounty from a redwood.

"Is this everyone?" I asked Marshall. He nodded. "We've gathered you all here tonight because we can't sit by and watch the atrocity that happened to Jeanette and do nothing. This label of 'scrawn' and 'breeder' is nothing more than Paul's demented way to control things. I mean, he thinks he can play god? He's nuts." I laughed in disgust.

Some of the women looked down; the rest remained silent. I wasn't sure if they were afraid of me or simply too scared to agree.

"Our plan is to get you out of here," Marshall said. "All the women."

"And go where?" Lillian interrupted.

"Crempshaw Camp." I smiled.

"How?" she nearly yelled. "That must be at least fifty miles away. And how do we know they'll take us in?"

"It's actually one hundred and twenty-seven miles. And we don't have any guarantee they'll accept us. But why would they turn us away? We're capable, we're smart, and after what we've been through, surely they'll offer us salvation. I mean, at least, I hope they will."

"No way." Lillian shook her head from side to side. "No way, at least we're alive here."

"Alive?" Marshall spat. "You call this living? You have no autonomy. What if you can't provide large children? Will you be destined to be murdered like the others? Tossed away like trash?"

Lillian's face darkened. "I . . . I . . . don't know."

"And what if you have large babies, but they grow up to be small men and women? Or hit their growth spurts too late? Will Paul release them as well?" I asked. "Plus, he's not even letting the children be raised here. Do you really want your toddler to be raised by the brutes at Kidwynn Camp? Because that's Paul's plan, and we've already seen it in action. How many of you in here have already had your children sent away? And for what, so they can train in lumberjacking from the time they can walk until they can make Paul money?"

"How do we know this isn't a trick?" Lillian asked.

A few of the women quietly murmured behind her.

Marshall looked confused. "What? Why would we lie about this?"

These women were so broken.

"How do we know this isn't a test from Lumberchief Paul?" Lillian stepped toward me.

I turned away and faced the scrawn. They looked even more frightened than the breeders. I closed my eyes and let out a sigh. "Because I'm a scrawn."

Lillian tilted her head to the side. "And? I could tell that when you walked in. What does that have to do with anything?" I could hear the anger growing in her voice.

"I'm not a scrawn man." I untucked my shirt. Marshall's eyes grew wide. "I'm a scrawn. Like you." I exposed my swollen belly.

A collective gasp rushed through the tent.

"Why?" Lillian asked. "Why would you come here? You've heard about the eugenics. Why come to a camp where you're doomed? And as a man? No one's that selfless. Why put you and your baby at risk? I don't understand."

"Because, well, I was here before." I removed my hat. No one flinched. "Oh right, I'm bald now. That was part of the disguise. Try to imagine me with long blonde hair."

"Annalise?" Lillian started crying. "I thought . . . I thought you . . . you died."

"Well, it wasn't for lack of trying," I said. I recounted my freak out, the mechanicals chasing me in the timber, my run-in with the keringer, and finally, Marshall. Speaking of Marsh and how he practically saved my life choked me up a bit. I blamed it on the hormones. "So yeah," I finished. "That's basically what's been happening. And now we have this wood mule, and we're going to get it fixed up. Marshall is going to provide the food and then we are out of here. No more deaths."

"Is everyone in?" Marshall asked.

Silence.

"I understand you're scared." I sat on a cot. "I do, but I promise you, I hate Paul more than any of you. I'm not working for him. This isn't a test."

"But he's your brother," a breeder said. "How could you hate him?"

Here it was. I had to tell them. I glanced at Marshall and felt guilty all over again. He'd always been my friend, but I knew this would break his heart. "I hate him because he killed the father of my baby. The heir to Younish Camp."

CHAPTER 24

Marshall stared forward, expressionless. I was flooded with questions.

"Lumberchief Walter was the father of your baby?"

"Paul killed him?"

"How?"

"I didn't know you two were together."

"Ladies," I said. "Keep it down. Do you want to get caught? Let me answer your questions one at a time. Yes, Walter and I dated for the last two years. We were in love. Obviously, we were private about it because he was still proving himself to his dad. Paul, as you know, was his best friend. Once Walter's father died, and he officially took over as lumberchief, Paul changed. For some deranged reason, I think Paul thought he was going to be the next lumberchief. Paul didn't think Walter was ready. Or maybe that he'd be better.

"Once Paul found out I was pregnant, he flipped. I can't exactly *prove* he killed Walter, but I know it. It was all too convenient. An accident where there are no witnesses? No way. And then he enacts a law, one that forbids me from having children. One that kills the only true heir to the camp? That has sabotage written all over it.

"I am not going to sit by and have anyone else suffer

because Paul wants to kill Walter's baby with the creation of an insane eugenics program."

Marshall stoked the wood in the stove and stood tall. "Who's in? Annalise has been very forthcoming. She's given you all the proof you need to know she's not a plant."

One by one, they all agreed.

I smiled. "Okay, I, uh, think Marshall has a few things we need to go over, and we can solidify the plan."

He avoided my eye contact. "The wood mule needs some repairs. Luckily, we have a mechanic in the scrawn group who can fix the engine. I'll sneak her out when I can—hopefully tomorrow or the next day. Then we'll need to attach an old canvas to the top to create shelter, so keep your eye out for an extra one. I have been rationing out food the last few days and drying meats and making flatbreads. I'll keep doing that until we leave and have enough food to get us to Crempshaw. I think we can get this done in five days."

"Five days?" someone exclaimed.

"Yeah." I tucked in my shirt. "In case you've forgotten, time is of the essence."

"You're right," Marshall said. "I'll do my best. We've already got enough pregnant women who are running out of time. And the last thing we need is Paul getting his wish and making one of the breeders pregnant too."

"Too late." A tall brunette studied the ground.

"No! Oh, no. I'm so sorry." Rage churned in my stomach. "This ends in five days or less."

"Okay," Lillian said.

"Now let's get these ladies back to their tent before someone notices they're gone."

CHAPTER 25

The one thing I loved about being pregnant was the sleep. For the first time in months, I was sleeping so soundly and deeply. That night, I dreamt of Walter. I hadn't dreamt of him in weeks. Talking about him last night must have unleashed a well of feelings I'd kept hidden away. My heart was full and happy for a brief moment before I was abruptly awoken by the morning bugle.

It jerked me from my sleep, and I sat straight up, then buried myself deep into my warm blanket. I yawned and immediately regretted it. The men's quarters smelled like one giant fart mixed with sour alcohol.

I tried to remember my dream, but it was fleeting, like trying to catch sand. My back ached and my ankles were swollen. Four more days—I could do this.

I had to do this.

Since I'd slept in my clothes, all that was left to do was lace up my boots and secure my suspenders. I kept my head down and made a beeline out of the smelly tent. I had to pee, and the men's latrine was obviously off limits. I hurried to the back of Paul's tent. It was perfect. He kept his sleeping quarters isolated away from the rest. Total privacy. And I got the gratification of pissing on his tent. After all he drank last night, a little trickle didn't wake him.

On the way to the mess hall, I opened my tin of peppermint to curb the nausea. The cool mint helped more than I had expected, but the urge to barf was still there. Like a sneeze that wouldn't quite erupt, but still made me uncomfortable.

I quickly walked through the line and grabbed my breakfast. A pair of eyes bored into me. I wanted to ignore them, but I couldn't. Marshall. My stomach dropped to the floor. The secret was out, and the sadness was written all over his face. Was he sad because he was jealous? Or just sad because my baby was never going to have a chance to meet its father? Perhaps he was just sad for me. For my situation. Knowing I was the reason Walter was dead. I blinked hard and looked away.

I needed to have a conversation with him, but I was going to avoid it for as long as possible. It was too much. Davious sat near me and babbled on about something. I ignored him and gobbled up my eggs so I could get the hell out of there.

Last night's events raced through my mind. Jeanette's blood-stained gown, the ax, and talking to the women. I had so much to deal with, and we were out of time. Failure wasn't an option. Not again.

The middle of camp was already crowded with jacks. It smelled of campfire and stale booze. Most rubbed their eyes or head, tired and hungover. Embers wafted into the air as they added more wood to the bonfire. I held out my hands, trying to warm them, waiting. Paul's daily orders couldn't come soon enough.

Four scrawn carried my dear brother on his elaborate throne. I gritted my teeth. His eyes were watery, face pale. No, green—his face was actually green—which gave an odd contrast to his icy-blue eyes. He sat slumped in his throne, half-awake.

He raised his arm; the crowd quieted.

"No work today," he mumbled. The crowd responded with a mixture of relief and grumbles. "Too dangerous. But I'll need a few of you to scout out the area. See if the keringer pit is still active or if it has moved on. Volunteers?"

He raised his head, then grabbed his forehead and grimaced.

"No one?" He waved his chainsaw arm. A scrawn quickly ran away and returned with a mug of ale. "You know what they say, hair of the dog." He took a sip and gagged.

"Serves him right," I mumbled.

He took a deep breath, hesitated, then downed the contents of the mug. "In addition"—he burped— "if the keringer has left, I'll need you to follow its tracks and see where it has moved, and report back to me."

Again, no one responded.

"Where's that guy? The new one?" Paul waved his cup to be refilled. "Didn't he see one or something?"

I ducked my head and pulled my beanie as low as it would go. Although he didn't really seem to remember what I told him, maybe I could still talk my way out of it if he cornered me.

"Alfred, or was it Arnold? No matter, the pay is double your daily wage," Paul said, sweetening the deal. Two men reluctantly raised their hands. I didn't recognize them; they must have been newer. "Off you go. The rest of you have the day off. Stay close. We can't risk losing anyone else. I'm sure most of you will want to catch up on your rest anyway. Where's Marshall?" He slurred his words. Great, he was drunk already. But how? I wasn't much of a drinker, but I guessed drinking so late into the night, then again so early, was the ticket to a constant buzz. "Someone find Marshall and tell him the potlatch will start early tonight, so plan dinner accordingly."

I wasn't sure if we were dismissed, so I waited around for a little bit. This was perfect—I had my out. Getting to the broken-down wood mule wouldn't be a problem today.

"Lumberchief Paul," someone yelled. "Will you be resting today?"

"Depends." Paul perked up. "What do you have in mind? I'm feeling much better."

"Davious wants to get grafted!"

Wide-eyed, I stared at Davious. He couldn't be serious. Maybe he was still drunk from the night before too. Davious smirked, arms crossed. I wasn't sticking around for this.

As I walked away, I heard Paul say, "Normally, we wait at least six months. But what the hell? Let's do it."

Now was my chance. I held my head high and walked out of camp through the small gap that had become my personal entrance and exit.

CHAPTER 26

The back side of camp was less populated, so I took the long way. It was safer and I could avoid the real entrance altogether. Hair on the back of my neck stood at attention. It felt like someone was following me. I couldn't shake the feeling. I shivered. My nerves were frayed, and I needed to calm down.

As I got closer, I stepped out of the brush and walked along the spires. A piercing scream followed by cheers stopped me in my tracks. They must have started the grafting process on Davious. I wondered which perfectly healthy limb they'd chosen to amputate and replace?

Idiots.

The mule looked just as broken down as the last time I'd seen it. I guess I'd hoped it would have magically fixed itself. I slowly walked around it and took a solid inventory of what needed fixing.

Another scream erupted from camp. More cheers. *That's odd. They usually pass out after the first incision. Davious must be stronger than I thought.*

The list of fixups on the wood mule wasn't as long as I had expected, but the infractions were big. And Paul starting the potlatch earlier than usual only complicated things more. Now I was stuck out here alone, no Marshall or his alleged crew to help with the repairs. I honestly didn't even know where to begin. The engine? No, that looked too difficult. The wheel? Maybe.

As I bent down to inspect an intact wheel, I heard a rustle in the timber. I cowered and hid myself completely behind it. If it was a keringer, I was toast. It would sniff me out, but I doubted it would come this close to camp. Not with all the screaming and commotion coming from the grafting ceremony.

Two steel-toed boots appeared in my line of view. I quietly grabbed a rusted pipe from the ground next to me. The footsteps stopped at the side of the wood mule. Damn. It wasn't just a passerby.

I tiptoed around the back; I was going to have to ambush the intruder. He was tall, and thick. I was no match for him.

I stepped on a branch and it snapped. The man spun around, hands balled into fists. Ready for a fight. His face was as red as his hair.

"Frank?"

CHAPTER 27

"Angus?" Frank's voice was colored with surprise.

"What the hell are you doing here?" I asked.

"I should ask you the same," he replied. "What are you . . .? Put down that pipe."

I dropped it to my side but kept a firm grip on it. "I asked first."

"It looks like I'm here for the same reason as you," he said, carefully.

"And what's that?" I asked.

"You seemed upset last night." He took a small step toward me. "At the releasing."

"So did you," I replied. I couldn't get a read on him.

"Of course, I was." He scratched his beard. "A woman . . . and that baby. It doesn't get any easier." He looked away.

"But you're not a scrawn. Why do you care?"

"What?" He laughed, but it sounded more like he was masking a sob. "You can't be serious."

"Aren't we just disposable?"

"I've been here at Younish for years," he started.

I'd seen Frank before, but never talked to him. No reason to.

"Things used to be different," he continued. "Better. I actually grew up here. This was my home, all I'd ever known. But ever since Lumberchief Walter died, things have changed." He bit his lip, seeming to be searching for the right thing to say. "I've never been grafted, as you can see."

"What's your point?" I asked.

"Are you planning an escape?" He crossed his arms.

"What?" I laughed. "Are you nuts? Oh, yeah, sure. I'll just hop on this broken mule and drive away."

Silence.

"Are you?" I asked. "Are you planning an escape?"

"Yes," he said flatly. "I'm forty-two. In eight years, I'll have aged out according to Scrawn Law and be banished. No one else does that. Every other camp says you can work as long as you like. I'm ready to defect. After what happened today, me and a few men are leaving."

"Really?" I asked. "Because Paul was hungover? *That's* your last straw? He's hungover all the time. That's nothing new." He looked at me quizzically. "I mean, that's what I've heard."

"How long have you been out here?"

"Today? I dunno, a few hours?"

"You missed it," he replied. "You missed the grafting."

I slowly nodded. *What's his end game?* "Self-mutilation isn't really my thing."

"He's dead." Frank's voice cracked. "Davious is dead."

"What?" I nearly yelled.

"They grafted all four limbs. Paul was drunk. He just kept going and going. It was gruesome. I tried to stop them. No one listened. Chopped him right up." He lowered his head. "I can't do it anymore. We lost a good man because of the lumberchief's insanity." He turned away from me, crouched, and buried his face in his hands.

It was now or never. Heck, he was going to take the mule as it was. Fessing up was the only chance I had.

"I'm sorry, Frank," I said. "And this mule needs a lot of work. I don't know how long it will take to get it up and running."

He stood and pressed his palms into his eyes. "Does that mean you're in? We can trust you?"

"About that," I said. "I was actually planning on leaving with Marshall."

"That's great," he said. "Marshall is a great kid."

"That's not all." I tossed my head back and stared at the gray sky. "I am taking all the women, breeders and scrawn alike."

He stroked his beard.

"What I saw last night was gruesome," I said. "I know I just joined, but no one should be forced to live like this. I heard Crempshaw is a four or five-day wagon ride away. But there are some old logging trails, so it shouldn't be too bad. I'm hoping they'll take us."

"The Gibson Trail?" Frank frowned. "I doubt anyone has used that in the last decade. It's very dangerous. Superstitious folks say it's cursed and will bring bad luck."

Great. Just perfect.

"I'm not superstitious," Frank added.

"Is there a better way?" I asked.

"Not unless you want to take a weeklong detour. It should be fine. You said the women are on board?" he asked.

"Yes," I said. "I talked to them last night."

"Then it sounds like we have a plan."

He held out his hand. I shook it. I prayed I wasn't making a mistake.

"We won't all fit on the mule, but we can take turns

riding and walking. I guess we better get to repairing the old girl." Frank kicked the broken wheel.

I pulled out my check list. "That's the problem. I don't know how long it will take." I handed him the paper. "We'd like to leave in four days. Five at the most. But look at all the repairs."

He studied the list. "It's actually not that bad. I have a few men who will be fleeing as well. We can work on it today since there's no logging." His eyes were still fixed on the paper. "Wait, rotted bed? When did that happen?" He pushed away the wet leaves and pine needles and exposed a canvas tarp covering the bed. He yanked it hard and exposed a perfectly sturdy deck.

"Oh," I said. "I just assumed it was rotten. I didn't realize preparations had been made to preserve it."

"It broke down a few years ago, but Lumberchief Walter made sure we still protected it. We never got around to fixing it." His voice was sad and distant. "Anyway, I'll grab my men. We'll push it into the timber and work on it in shifts today and into the night. Hopefully, we'll have it done today or tomorrow."

"Really?" I asked. "I'll tell Marshall. We'll get the food ready. Maybe we'll get out even sooner." I smiled. "No one will ever be released again."

CHAPTER 28

Naturally, I found Marshall in the kitchen along with the rest of the cooks. I nodded toward the direction of the barrels and waited for him.

"Where have you been?" Marshall pushed the flap of the tent behind him. "I tried looking for you."

"I snuck out to work on the wood mule," I said. "It's so weird being a guy here. I snuck out, but I know I didn't *have* to. Being a man . . . you get different freedoms. No one is bothering me day in and day out about cleaning those damn blankets. Once work is over, we party. As a woman, we never got time off. We're under constant scrutiny, and when they don't need us, we're banished to our tent. I can't wait to get out of here."

"Trust me, it's not all that great. Not for all men, anyway." Marshall fixed his gaze toward the ground. "You said you worked on the mule—how'd it go?"

"Better than I expected." I crossed my arms in front of my chest.

"Where's the list?" He crouched, ensuring he was fully hidden. "I can divvy up what needs to get done with the women in a little bit."

"Well," I said. "That's the thing. Frank caught me."

"What?" Marshall took an involuntary step back and pinched the bridge of his nose.

"Yeah." I forced a laugh. "He was pretty upset."

Marshall cursed. "We have to go; we'll come back for the women. Come on." He grabbed my hand.

I froze. My heart raced. His dark complexion magnified the cracks on his worn knuckles. "Marsh." I paused, and gently pulled my hand back. "He's on our side. Did you hear about Davious?"

"On our side? What are you talking about?" he asked. "Davious. Yes. It's despicable. He bled out. It was horrible, and he was conscious right until . . . Well, you know, until the end."

"Oh." I shuddered. "That explains why Frank was so shaken up about it."

"Anna." He stood. "We need to talk, let's go to the supply tent."

I nodded and led the way. The potlatch was in full swing. Walking through unnoticed was a breeze for the moment. Marshall, ever careful, stayed a few steps behind me. The moldy smell of the supply tent was like a slap in the face the moment I walked in. I found an old barrel to sit on and waited for Marshall.

"What is going on?" he asked the moment he burst through the flap doors.

"Frank is horrified. He and a few of his men want out," I said. I recounted our conversation. I told him how he never liked Paul, how he refused to get grafted, and that I trusted him.

"Anna." Marshall's face contorted into an angry frown. "Now we have additional mouths to feed. Huge men. And less spots on the wagon. This isn't good."

"Did you hear me, Marsh?" I asked. "They can fix the wood mule. Hopefully by the end of the day. That's awesome news."

"We already had someone who could fix the engine."

"Yeah." I stood. "And what about the wheel, and the other structural stuff? Besides, you know we couldn't have worked on it so close to camp. We would have gotten caught. Frank and his men moved it into the timber."

"How do you know he didn't just turn you in?" Marshall released a frustrated breath. "Damn it, Anna! You're so reckless sometimes."

That speared deep into my soul. Tears welled up in my eyes. I turned, blinking them away. "What is this really about?" I turned on my heel and stalked toward him. "Huh? Tell me. You and I both know Frank's help will be paramount."

"It's exactly what I said." His voice was overly calm and emotionless. "You could have ruined the whole plan."

I stepped toward him until we were toe to toe. "Tell me, Marsh. Come on, let's hear it. Why are you really mad?"

Nothing.

I pushed him on his hard chest. "Is this what you want?" I asked. "You want to fight? Will that make you feel better?"

He took a step back and crossed his arms across his greasy apron.

I pushed him again. "Talk to me!" I couldn't fight it anymore. Tears flowed freely and stained my dirty face.

"Be quiet," he yelled.

"Marshall, you've been weird ever since last night," I cried.

He looked away.

"Fine." I sniffled. "I'll say it. Walter was my lover. Yes, I *loved* him. He's the father of my baby. Why did that information change anything? I'm just as knocked up today as I was yesterday."

"I don't know." He started pacing. "Because, Anna, we were friends. Best friends. And you hid this from me. Why? I thought you trusted me."

"I did trust you. I mean, I *do* trust you. I just, I don't know. It was complicated . . ." I trailed off. "What else?"

"I'm terrified for you! You"—he pointed to my belly—"and it are everything Paul wants gone. That baby holds the bloodline to this camp. Anna, even *if* we escape, what are you going to do? Raise a baby by yourself in a new camp? It has the right to know who its father was. When the truth comes out, Paul will come for the kid."

"I'll tell the little ankle biter when the time is right. And I've got some time. I hear babies aren't born with the ability to communicate with words."

"Stop it, Anna." He held my shoulders. "You know this is serious. All those women are loyal to you now, because they need out. But once we're at Crempshaw . . . They're going to steer clear of you. You're dangerous."

"I know," I whispered.

"I want to help you," he said.

"You have helped me." I pulled off my beanie. "You saved my life."

"That's not what I meant." He dropped a hand from my shoulder and tipped my chin up. He stared at me. "I want to help you and the baby."

"You're crazy," I said. "You know how this could end."

"Anna, I'm not letting you go through this alone."

"Yeah, well . . ." My voice cracked. "Let's just wait until we cross that bridge."

He was right. My baby was a ticking time bomb. If, heck, *once* Paul found out I was alive, the bounty on my head and this baby's head was going to be huge. I'd already come to the realization I might have to find someone else to raise it, give it a new identity. But if Marshall was willing to help me, maybe I'd have a chance.

Maybe.

Marshall wrapped his arms around me. I broke down. I had deluded myself into thinking if I made it out, everything would be okay. Maybe saving the other women hadn't been purely altruistic, but rather a distraction. But Marshall held a mirror up to my face, and I was forced to see my situation for how dire it truly was. I cried until his shirt was wet.

I was in so much trouble.

"Anna." Marshall released me from his warm embrace. "You have to get it together for a minute."

"Right." I wiped my nose with my sleeve.

"Do you think you can look through the extra supplies in here?"

"Yeah." I shoved my beanie back on my head. "What do we need?"

"A tent for the cover on the mule. I guess some blankets, and a few poles to hold up the tent."

I pointed to the corner. "Yes, I'll put them over here. And let Frank know. His men can load them up. They've been here longer. No one will question them moving supplies. Especially with the party raging out in the common area."

It was mid-afternoon, but the potlach made it seem like it was late in the day. The music was loud and the booze flowed.

"Okay," Marshall said. "I've got to get back to the kitchen before anyone comes looking for me. I'll see if I can steal more rations for the extra people."

"Right."

He turned to walk out, stopped, and looked over his shoulder. "I meant what I said."

I gave him the best half-smile I could muster and waited for him to leave. The moment he was out, I was once again a girl posing as a boy on a mission. I'd deal with my feelings later.

Random poles were scattered in a corner. I lined a few of the non-rusted ones up and found two longer ones that were roughly the same size. I lucked out when I found a smaller set that actually matched. Now it was time to hunt down some tents.

Jackpot—I found a stack hidden behind an old stove. Opening and inspecting them for holes proved to be a bigger task than I anticipated. They were heavy, dirty, and large. Huge spiders scurried away each time I unfolded a flap. A lamp toppled over when I spread one out, and it shattered. The party outside raged, so I wasn't worried about them hearing me.

The blankets were the easy part. Seeing as how I used to launder them daily for the jacks, I was an expert in the area. In fact, I actually knew where Paul's secret stash was kept. His wool blankets were much nicer than the rest. I'd sneak those out later. In fact, I decided I would take all his blankets. A smile spread across my face.

A loud scream wiped my grin away. It was a terrified scream.

From a woman.

CHAPTER 29

I peeked out the flap and saw a woman being forcefully carried, headed right toward me. I recognized her immediately and rushed in her direction. Ruby. A pregnant scrawn. But she was only a few months further in her pregnancy than me. Maybe six months pregnant at the most.

Two men held up her shoulders and another held her leg. Her free leg kicked wildly, and she screamed. What was going on?

One of the men eyed me. *Oh no, did she rat me out?* My pulse raced. This couldn't be happening.

"You," the man who eyed me said. "Grab her leg."

I shook my head in confusion. "Wh-what?"

"Grab her leg."

Ruby looked at me desperately. I didn't understand. "What's going on?"

The potlatch quieted and he yelled, "She's early—this one is in labor. Looks like we gots anuther releasin'!"

"No." I took a step back. I disappeared back into the tent and collapsed onto the ground. How was this happening? There was nothing I could do. It wasn't supposed to happen like this. No. We were supposed to leave, together. Safe. I buried my face into the canvas tent and screamed. I screamed again and again until my voice was raw.

I lay on my back. My throat ached. I had to do something. *Frank*. We had to leave tonight. Dizziness fell over me the moment I stood, and I steadied myself on a stump.

The canvas flap rustled in the cold evening air. I could see people headed toward the bonfire. I made a run for it and was through my secret exit in no time. I ran hard. Cold air rushed into my lungs, my sore calf burned, and I welcomed the pain. It was nothing compared to what Ruby was experiencing.

Unsure of where Frank had moved the wood mule, I stopped at its last location.

"Frank," I whispered. "Frank!"

Trees rustled behind me and I swung around. A lantern caught my eye first. "Angus?"

"Yeah, yep, it's me," I said.

The lantern swung back and forth as Frank made his approach toward me. Once he was in sight, he motioned his hand at me. "Get over here. You're going to blow our hiding spot."

"Sorry." I jogged toward him and followed him into a clearing. "How's it coming?"

"Almost done. I figure we'd break for the night and come back early tomorrow."

"No way," I said. "We can't wait. Can you finish it tonight?"

"Maybe." He furrowed his brow. "We're tired. And—" He must have seen the look on my face. "What happened?"

"It's Ruby." I looked away. "A scrawn. She's in early labor. They're going to release her and the baby tonight. We have to get out of here as fast as we can. We can't wait for someone else to go into labor."

"Men." He turned away from me. Three lumberjacks were barely illuminated by dimly lit lanterns. "Let's push through. We'll finish tonight. There's going to be another releasing."

"If you don't mind," I said, "I'll just wait here for a little bit longer. I don't want to witness another death."

Frank nodded and walked back to the wood mule. "Do the others know we're leaving tonight?"

"No." I blinked hard. "Okay, I'll go back. Listen, we'll meet here right after midnight. Everyone from the potlatch will either be passed out or too drunk to notice. Okay? I'll bring the supplies with Marshall."

"No. I'll come to you," he said. "I'll back the mule up to the fence. There's a hole near the mess hall."

"They might hear us," I said.

"Angus." Frank held the lantern up to his face. "Look, I know you want to be the hero here, but you cannot sneak out all those women and supplies and drag them out here. Some of those women must be ready to pop. Plus, it'll take hours to get everything loaded."

"Fine," I said. "But if this thing starts up and is too loud, we're switching to my plan."

"I've already tested it," he said. "We'll be fine."

* * *

I ran back to camp. Screams, cheers, and cries echoed throughout the forest. I knew what was happening, but I pushed it out of my mind. Pretending it wasn't happening was all I had in that moment. Plus, I needed to find Marshall.

"Marshall!" I burst into the kitchen area of the mess hall. Several cooks stopped and stared at me. The kitchen smelled like onion and spiced meat. "Paul, uh, Lumber-chief Paul needs to speak to you. Come with me."

"Should we keep cooking, boss?" someone asked him.

"Yes." He wiped his hands on a towel. "I'll let you know if there are any change requests."

We walked back to the barrels, our regular rendez-vous point.

"I'm sorry," I said. "I figured you'd be alone, that they'd all be at the releasing."

His face darkened. "It's already over."

"Already?" I asked.

He looked away.

"Oh. But they were just cheering. Poor Ruby . . ." I trailed off.

"If it's any comfort"—he crouched next to me—"the baby wasn't right. She wasn't alive at birth."

"She? Ruby had a little girl."

Marshall studied the ground. A few colorful leaves dotted the brown dirt.

"Did they spare Ruby's life?" My voice perked up.

"No." His voice was low. "Paul said he was doing the camp a service. This was exactly why they needed to have a breeding program. To 'clean out' the gene pool. People are more convinced than ever about it."

"We can't stay," I said.

"I know," he replied.

"I checked on Frank; they'll be done tonight. We can't risk another early labor. Tonight. We leave tonight."

"Anna." He paused and scanned the area. "I don't have enough rations ready for the trip. Especially with the extra mouths to feed."

"We'll make do!" I shot up and stood tall. "We'll hunt. And we can steal extra stuff. They'll already know we're gone first thing in the morning, why not take tomorrow's rations?"

"I'll do my best," he said.

"Okay, we're all meeting at our entrance just after midnight. I guess a few others know about that spot. I thought it was just mine."

"Fine." He nodded once.

"I'll let both sets of women know. They can stay in their tent until I come get them."

"How will we be carrying our supplies to the tent?"

"Frank is backing the wagon up close to us to save time."

"Won't it be too loud?" He cocked his head to the side.

"Frank says no. I'm going to place the tent, poles, and blankets outside now. Save a little time, you know?"

Marshall's dark eyes held my gaze. "We're really doing this, aren't we, Anna?"

"We don't have a choice."

CHAPTER 30

I decided to test my luck with the canvas tent. It was cumbersome, but less so than the poles. About fifteen feet away was a horde of drunk lumberjacks, laughing and throwing dice. How could they party after watching Ruby and her baby's release? After Davious's completely unnecessary death? In the short time Paul had been the lumberchief, he had managed to shift their moral compass to a terrifying direction and attracted the worst kind of men.

I casually walked to the back of camp and tossed the tent through the hole. A small sense of relief washed over me. Almost everyone was at the bonfire in the middle of camp. There were only a few men scattered about my area, mostly drunk and stumbling, or already passed out. It was easier than I expected to make the trek back and forth undetected. As long as I took a slightly different route each time, no one seemed to notice me. Or if they did, they didn't care. With that task finished, I needed to talk to the women.

It was getting late, and that meant the scrawn women would be in the men's sleeping quarters turning down their cots for the night. A job I hated and had done many, many times. I stepped in, and Elizabeth rushed over to me.

"Anna," she gasped. "It's Ruby! She's gone. They—"

"Shh," I said. "And it's *Angus*. I know, I heard what happened. We've changed the plan."

The women gathered around me. "We're leaving tonight. Finish your job here and go back to your tent. Once everything is loaded and we're ready to go, I'll come get you. It'll be after midnight. Rest up, it's going to be a long night."

"Tonight?" Elizabeth said. "Are you sure? How?"

"Yes," I said. "There's been another change. Frank. You may already know him; he and three other jacks are leaving with us. In fact, they repaired the old wood mule today."

The women murmured. Even the prospect of getting away wasn't enough to make them smile.

"Get back to work, I have a few things I need to grab," I said. "We'll be together soon."

I left and jogged toward the breeders' tent. In the short time I'd been with the scrawn, the party had grown. Men who'd passed out earlier were now awake and drinking again. Save for the random straggler outside the main bonfire, the camp was empty. Except for the guard outside the breeders' tent. I cursed under my breath. This was problematic, because I'd need to convince him he was off again, and it would be even more difficult since he was probably stone-cold sober.

I walked up to the tartan-clad man. "Well, I'm back for my shift."

"What?" he asked. "Again?"

"Yep." I shoved my hands in my pockets to keep them from shaking. "There was another releasing. The lumberchief thinks we might not have to even guard the tent after today. The baby was wrong." I held back tears. "No one doubts the validity of the breeding program now. And certainly, no man will violate it." I choked on the last few words.

"Violate?" His face twisted with confusion.

Why was size the only thing that mattered to Paul? This guy was an idiot, but his stature allowed him to pass on his genes. "Disobey. Break. I don't know how else to dumb this down for you." I clapped the back of his right shoulder and gently pushed him forward. "It means you can go join the potlatch."

He turned toward me, and with a lopsided grin, he shrugged his shoulders and walked away.

Most of the women were already in bed. A few gasped when I burst into the tent, and some yanked their blankets high up around their chins.

Lillian sighed with relief. "Ruby," she started.

"I know," I interrupted. "That's why I'm here."

"What can you do?" Hazel interjected. Her words were harsh. She was young, maybe seventeen at most. Her long, curly brown hair was still wet from her evening shower. "Can you bring Ruby back? No. This whole convoluted plan was a waste."

Eight pairs of angry eyes stared me down.

"Are you kidding me? How is this my fault?" I furrowed my brow.

"He's your brother," Lillian said. "Maybe you're sick in the head too."

"Exactly." Hazel stood. "Is this a test? Did Lumberchief Paul put you up to it?"

I blinked hard and tossed my head back, stretching my tired neck muscles. Were they serious? I understood why they were so scared—heck, I was just as fearful. But I was their only lifeline.

"Does this look like a test?" I slid my suspenders off

my shoulders, untucked my shirt, and exposed my burgeoning belly again.

"What does that prove?" Hazel asked. "We know you're pregnant. You've shown us before. I don't trust you."

I unlaced my boot and pulled the bottom of my pants up to my knee. "See this?" I pointed to the healing gash in my leg. "I was impaled by a freaking branch when I ran away! Is this fake?"

No one responded.

"Look, I get that you're scared. I'm scared too. We don't have time for this." I shook my head. "We're leaving tonight. We can't risk anyone else going into early labor."

"Tonight?" Lillian's eyes were wide with surprise.

"Yes." I clamped my lips shut. "There's another thing. I have a friend, Frank, he's a lumberjack. He and his three friends helped fix the wood mule. They want out too. We need the extra hands and they're strong."

"What?" Hazel said. "If you're not a mole, then he probably is! You expect us to not only trust you, but him too?"

Breathe, I told myself. *Do not yell at them. They're scared. Powerless.* I tucked my pants into my boot, laced it up, tucked in my shirt, and pulled up my suspenders. "Yes," I said evenly.

"Well, I don't." Hazel's voice was high-pitched, and she was practically yelling.

"You know what? Fine. Don't trust either of us. I don't care. But don't hinder our escape. If you want to stay and be forced to breed with morons, go ahead. Be my guest. For those who want a chance at living a normal life, we will be leaving tonight. Either myself or Marshall will be back around midnight. Pack what you need, but don't bring much. We don't have a lot of room. Also, rest as much as you can. Like I said, it's going to be a long night." I stormed out before they could ask questions.

Like every other plan in my life, this one was falling apart.

Everything had gone from well-planned to hell in a handbasket in a matter of hours.

CHAPTER 31

To say I was frustrated was an understatement. The women were suspicious of my motives. The scrawn were completely defeated. Ruby had been murdered. Her baby died. I had no idea if my plan was even going to work. My stupid leg still ached. And where the hell was Marshall?

"I'm right here."

I looked up. "Huh?"

"Anna," Marshall said. "Why are you talking to yourself? Are you okay?"

I didn't realize I'd spoken those words out loud. "Why is everyone suddenly concerned with my mental health?" I kicked a rock. "I'm just annoyed. This plan is falling apart. I think they thought they were saved when I first told them of our evacuation plan. Ruby's death changed all of that. They're frightened, don't trust me, and worst of all, I think the scrawn"—I cringed. I needed to lose that word from my vocabulary—"have lost their spirit. They seem so hopeless."

"Can you blame them? The last few months, their lives have been hell. *You* of all people know that. Anyway, we can't worry about that right now." Marshall heaved a bag of rice from his shoulder onto the ground. Dust particles wafted into the air. "I've got almost all the rations outside the camp. Here, take this." He pushed the burlap bag toward me. "I'll meet you back here, and we can move the rest out this way."

The heavy bag over my shoulder made me feel useful and distracted me for the moment. I met Marshall seven or eight times over the next hour, until we had a large pile of food and water outside the perimeter of camp. We rested against the hard wooden spires just outside camp and sat in silence. The potlatch carried on into the night and seemed to get louder as the drinks flowed.

"What time is it?" I stared at the stars.

"Almost midnight," Marshall said.

"Where is Frank? We should be loaded up by now. The women are going to flip out." I closed my eyes, too tired to go searching for him.

Branches snapped, small trees fell, and a loud engine announced Frank's arrival. I jumped to my feet. Frank backed up the clunky wood mule while Marshall directed him in. The engine sputtered and finally turned off.

"Could you be any louder?" I asked. "I thought you said it would be quiet?"

"That *is* quiet." Frank stroked his beard. "Most mules are substantially louder than this."

I rubbed my hands down my face. "We're going to get caught."

Marshall was already handing supplies up to one of the jacks on the mule. The other was picking up supplies and bringing them to Frank.

"Wait," I said. "There are only three of you. Where's the fourth?"

"That's why we're late," Frank said. "We went back into camp to retrieve a few things. I think Stephen must have gotten caught up in the party or got cold feet. We looked for him and waited as long as we could."

"What?" I cursed. *He better not be ratting us out.*

Marshall walked up to me. "Angus." He placed his hands on my shoulders. "Go get the women. We'll have the wagon loaded by the time you get back. Hurry." He could hide the worry in his voice, but he couldn't hide the fear in his eyes. Not from me anyway.

It was my turn to be the strong one. I didn't dare bring up Hazel's trepidation. "Okay, Marsh. No problem."

I slipped back into camp and ran in the shadows to the scrawn tent. They were all lying in their beds, though I doubted any of them were sleeping. "Ladies," I whispered. "It's go time." They quickly rose and followed me out of the tent.

The seven women followed me toward the breeder tent. "Wait here, behind this shed," I said. "I'll be right back." Unsure of how this was going to play out, I didn't want them in earshot of the tent, nor did I want to expose them in case I had been outed.

I checked my surroundings once more for onlookers and stepped into the tent. They were all awake, waiting for me.

"You're late." Lillian smiled. "We've been waiting for you."

"Everyone?"

"Yes." Lillian turned toward Hazel. "Right?"

"Yeah." She had her hands on her hips and gave me a death stare. "I don't trust you or your brother."

"Look, I hate him as much as you. You have to see that." I sighed and turned to the rest of the women. "We have to be quick. Follow me, and stay quiet."

We filed out of the tent and met up with the scrawn. Sixteen women leaving the camp was risky, and we didn't have a moment to waste. I led them through long shadows. My heart thumped the inside of my ribcage. Some-one sniffled.

I cringed at the sobbing. I didn't blame them. We needed to get farther away so we weren't heard. Luck-ily, the potlatch carried on in the center of camp. Banjos strummed loudly, people laughed, and the low murmur of constant conversation hummed steadily.

The women hurried through my secret exit. One by one, they squeezed through.

"Me first!" Hazel cut to the front of the line.

"Fine, whatever." I pushed her through. "Just go!"

"Shh!" someone said.

A few of them looked around wildly, just waiting to get caught before it was their turn. A few crouched, trying to hide. Lillian paused and nodded at me before passing through.

"I don't know if I'll fit." A heavily pregnant woman looked up at me with red-rimmed eyes. "Don't let me hold you up."

"Nonsense." I directed her through sideways and pulled on one of the logs. "See?"

I was the last to squeeze through. I stared at the hole for a moment. When Walter first showed me the hole he'd made for us, it brought me such joy. Now it brought me happiness in a different way. It had become not only my secret way in and out, but also savior to us all. In a way, Walter had given me the tools to save myself. And our baby.

I paused, staring at the women, arms wrapped around each other, quiet tears flowing. Months of forced segre-gation were finally over. No scrawn. No breeders. Just scared and tired women.

"There's no time for this," Frank said.

Harriet shuddered. I felt her fear. Frank was still a jack, after all.

"All the pregnant women, on the mule," he ordered. "The rest of us will take turns walking and riding."

"He's right," I said. "Let's load up."

Frank fed the engine a heap of wood and started it. Nothing.

I swallowed hard. "Come on," I whispered. "Come on."

The engine sputtered. Marshall looked at me desperately. I shook my head. How was this happening? Frank promised me it was fixed. I hid my face in my hands, away from the stares of the other women.

Finally, I felt the engine turn over and roar to life, a bear of a machine. The mule moved. This was nothing like my last escape. We had a plan, food, and all the women. I—no, *we*—took *our* first steps toward freedom.

And this time, I wasn't in a flimsy nightgown.

CHAPTER 32

Late fall in the northern woods brought bone-biting cold. But the cold didn't bother me in the early hours of the day. I welcomed it. It was the feeling of freedom. The temperature kept me alert and awake. The sky faded from black into pale purples, and eventually, the sun broke the horizon and cast shades of oranges and reds through the trees.

After another hour or so, I was desperate for a break and switched spots with someone who'd been on the wagon. Marshall took over Frank's job of holding the throttle. I leaned against the side of his legs.

"Marsh?" I asked.

"Yeah?"

"Did we really pull this off?" I laughed—it was almost a hysterical, insane laugh, but a chuckle nonetheless.

"For now." His hand gently brushed my cheek. "Take a quick nap, Anna. Don't forget, you're pregnant too."

I tried to protest but the exhaustion won. I had a fitful sleep and dreamt of Paul finding us, releasing us one by one. It was one of those dreams where you knew you were asleep but couldn't wake yourself up. I awoke trying to catch myself. Was I falling? No, just confused by my surroundings. I felt the entire mule lean to the left. Over my shoulder, I saw we'd gone around a young tree that was too big to drive over.

We were coming to a stop; it was time for me to give up my spot to someone else. Even though I was pregnant, I didn't stay on the mule much. I hadn't revealed my gender, identity, or my condition to Frank and his friends yet. And quite honestly, I didn't feel like getting into it. It almost felt trivial at this point. We had bigger fish to fry.

Judging by the sun, it must have been ten or eleven. I'd slept a few hours, which was more than I'd planned on resting. Marshall jumped off the side before me and offered me a hand down. I rolled my eyes and jumped down just as he had. It did nothing for my calf, and everything for my pride.

He followed me as I walked to the other side of the wagon. I inspected the repaired wheel.

"It still looks solid," I said. "Do you think it'll last the entire trip?"

"I think so." He lightly kicked it in a few spots. "Frank's been a lumberjack his whole life. I'm sure he's repaired many wheels over the years."

"Why are we still stopped?" I asked. "We need to keep going."

"We need to eat." Marshall clapped his hands together.

He rummaged through some of the supplies and walked over to where Frank and his men had started a small fire. He cracked several eggs into a cast-iron pan. My stomach rumbled once I caught a whiff of it.

"Everything else we eat after today will be either dried meat or grain," Marshall announced. "No more fresh eggs. I figured these would keep overnight, so eat up."

We all got in line, and he evenly distributed the food amongst our crew of twenty-one. I was last in line, and we split what was left. I sat on a downed log next to Marshall.

"I bet they're going to be furious when they realize how much food you stole." I laughed.

Marshall didn't respond. He finished his eggs and started collecting plates.

"Load up," Frank said. "Marshall, why don't you stay on throttle duty; I'd like to walk a little longer."

Marshall nodded. The Gibson Trail certainly hadn't been traveled by anything with wheels in a very long time. Pine straw covered the dirt road, which helped conceal our tracks. Newly sprouted trees littered the path. Our heavy wheels rolled over the young saplings. Large ones, we drove around. Downed logs and both large and small rocks made for tricky maneuvering.

I studied the women. They were weary. We hadn't been traveling twelve hours, and they looked like we'd been traveling twelve days. Maybe they'd feel better after a proper night's rest.

I felt someone on the left of me. Frank.

"So," I said awkwardly. "Do you think they've noticed we're gone yet?"

"Maybe," he replied. "But without Marshall ringing the bell for breakfast, I'm sure they all slept in. They're probably just getting up now."

Frank kicked an overgrown bush.

"Don't you think the other cooks would have gotten up and cooked without Marshall?" I asked.

"I doubt it," he said. "Marshall was sick a few weeks ago and took the morning off. Since he wasn't there to wake them up, we had to skip breakfast."

I'd forgotten about that day. Or maybe I blocked it out. Paul made an example of one of the cooks. He tied him up, defenseless, while the angry jacks beat him to a bloody pulp. I shuddered.

"What do you think Paul will do once he notices?" Dry pine straw crunched under my feet.

"Oh, he'll come after us." Frank stroked his beard. "I'm sure he's furious. We destroyed his breeding program. The one thing we have on our side is that potlatch last night. If I know Paul, he'll be too hungover to leave camp for at least another hour or two. Plus, they'll have to figure out what to do for provisions. I assume Marshall took all the dried meat and breads."

"I think he did," I said. "I wish Paul would just accept that we defected and carry on." But I knew better. Paul was a vengeful man. There was no way he'd let us just walk out. Somehow, I hadn't been too worried about the consequences until now. Maybe because there was no way to avoid them. "Ugh, he's terrible. He's always been a little off, but never in my wildest dreams did I think that psycho would do something as horrible as a eugenics program that included killing women and babies."

"What?" Frank said. "Always been a little off? You've only been at camp a few days."

I pinched my nose between my eyes. "Frank, there's something I need to tell you." I took off my hat and faced him. He stopped and stared at me blankly. "Oh right, shaved head," I said. "I keep forgetting." I bashfully put my hat back on. "Imagine me with long hair."

Frank tilted his head and squinted his eyes.

"Frank, I'm Annalise, Paul's sister." I recounted my escape, subsequent return, and how Marshall and I planned to save all the women.

He stared forward, face emotionless, and walked.

"Frank." I stepped over a log. "Are you mad?"

"No," he said. "I'm not mad. That word isn't strong enough."

"I'm sorry," I said. "I didn't know how to tell you. And honestly, it never really came up."

"Never came up?" A muscle ticked in his jaw. "You can't be serious."

"That's not what I meant." I stepped in front of him and stopped. "There was just so much going on—the escape, the planning, fixing the mule. It didn't seem prudent."

"Didn't seem prudent?" he yelled. "I thought you were good, like us. Turns out you are just as self-serving as your brother."

The words stung.

"That's not fair," I said. The caravan had now passed us, and we were alone. "If I were self-serving, I would have just escaped on my own. Left everyone else behind."

"You came back because you were injured—you needed us."

"That's true," I started. "But after I was healed, I could have just stolen what I needed and left on foot. Paul wouldn't have cared, since I was Angus, a lowly scrawn."

Frank said nothing.

"I wanted to save those women. If I were truly as selfish as you think me, I wouldn't have risked my life and my baby's—"

"Baby?" he asked, eyes wide and angry.

I blinked hard. "I'm pregnant too."

"Well, this just keeps getting better."

"I'm sorry," I said. "You're right, I should have told you. But here we are. We've escaped. We're on our way to Crempshaw and a better life. Please, Frank, you don't have to like me, but please forgive me. I need you. We need you."

He relaxed his face and walked quickly in the direction of the wood mule.

"Frank—"

"You're not a drunk?" Frank interrupted.

"What? No, what are you talking about?"

"The hangovers."

"Oh, yeah." I cleared my throat. "Morning sickness. I figured that was a good cover."

"That's a relief," he said.

"A relief? How exactly is that a relief?"

"I was worried a drunk was leading us." He tried to laugh. "Here I thought you just had a beer belly and were perpetually hungover."

"Yeah," I said. "Can we please move past this?"

"I don't really have a choice," he said. "I'm too tired to stay upset. And, like you said, we're already this far in—what can I do about it now?"

"That reminds me," I said. "I haven't had morning sickness the last few days. Maybe I'm finally past that part."

"Let's hope," he responded coolly. "I'm going to tell Tommy and Brad." He picked up his pace to a slow run.

"Wait," I said. "Shouldn't I be the one to tell them?"

"No," he said. "Trust me on this."

I nodded and he ran up ahead.

We walked for hours. The sun moved up to the center of the cloudy sky. It wouldn't be long before it started its descent. Marshall and Frank traded places several times. I took another break and sat next to Marshall while he was on throttle duty. My tender feet protested as I made my way around the mule, checking on the women—which was harder than expected given the rough terrain and old wheels. I bounced and tripped my way through. Most were fine, all things considered. A few were motion sick, but the ones who were mentally broken were the worst. I didn't know how to help them.

I crouched next to a heavily pregnant woman. She was petite, at least three inches shorter than me. "How are you?" I brushed her tangled hair out of her face.

"I'm uncomfortable." She shifted, face grimaced. "This road is so rough."

She wasn't wrong, and frankly, she was generous calling it a road. Every few feet, someone would nearly get bucked off. If it wasn't large rocks we either had to go around or drive over, it was the overgrown brush and budding trees. The big bumps weren't the worst of it—they sucked but you could brace yourself. The hardest part was the constant jostling. I wasn't near as far along as some of the other women, so I could only imagine it made them feel like it was going to trigger labor. Or make them pee. Either way, it was miserable.

"Try to rest," I said. "I know it's bumpy, but you're off your feet."

"Wait until you're near the end." She glanced at my stomach.

"That bad?"

"It's not just that." She closed her eyes and grimaced. "I think I'm having cramps. The ones that prepare you for labor."

My eyes widened. "Labor?"

She cleared her throat. "Don't worry about me. I'm out of that awful camp. No matter what, I'm safe." She rested her hand on mine.

A man screamed.

The wagon came to an abrupt halt.

CHAPTER 33

"Marsh!" I yelled. "What happened?"

He cradled his arm. His lips were tucked into his mouth, and his eyes were squeezed shut.

"Let me look." I reached for him.

"No," he said. "I'm okay. I'm okay. It's just a little burn."

Frank had boarded the wagon by now. "Steam burn?"

"Yes," Marshall replied.

"Seen it a hundred times." Frank examined Marshall's arm. "These damn steam engines are dangerous." He picked up a rag off the wooden floor and tightly wrapped Marshall's arm. "Keep the compression on there; we'll clean it when we come across a clear stream. You'll be okay."

"Thanks," Marshall said.

"I'll take over for now," Frank said. "You're off throttle duty until further notice."

Marshall nodded, and he stepped down from the wagon.

"Marsh," I started.

"I'm fine," he snapped. "It just hurts, but it'll be fine. Come on, we're holding up the caravan."

We gave up our spots and walked in silence for the rest of the day. The steam engine sputtered and quit over and over. Time wasn't on our side; we had a woman possibly in labor, and a psycho back at camp who might or might not be coming after us.

The wood mule sputtered and groaned loudly to a complete stop.

"Crap!" I pulled on the sides of my non-existent hair. "Can you fix it?"

"Nothing to fix," Frank said. "We just need to get her moving, and the engine will turn over. I've seen this in the timber when the ground is too soft. Or steep. Or rough. Wood mules can be . . . fickle."

"Great. Everyone off," I yelled. "Can a few of you run up that hill and look to see if you see Paul?"

"I will," Elizabeth said, then jogged up the knoll.

"Marshall, you're lighter than me." Frank nodded toward the engine in the middle of the deck. "Try turning it back on once we get moving."

Marshall hopped on and took his spot behind the engine without a word.

We all lined up behind the mule and waited for direction. I let Frank lead the way since he had experience with it, and I had a feeling he was still pissed at me, and the last thing he wanted to hear was my voice.

"When I say *heave,* you push; when I say *ho,* let up and get ready to push. And watch your feet. Don't get behind a wheel," Frank shouted. "Heave! Ho! Heave! Ho!"

The heavy wood mule barely budged. We pushed and released, pushed and released. It rocked a tiny bit forward then back.

"Keep going," Frank grunted. I was thankful we'd gotten our rhythm and that he stopped yelling *heave, ho* at us. "It's moving now!"

I rammed my shoulder into it, and the thin wheels finally made half a revolution.

"Again!" Frank yelled. "Don't let off this time!"

I watched as the spokes on the wheel rolled forward and continued.

"Now, Marshall." Frank's face was bright red, and a vein bulged in his neck.

I felt the engine roar to life, followed by cheers.

"Yes!" I turned to Frank. "Nice work."

"For now," he said. "We'll have to keep it at an even pace to keep it from happening again." He turned to the group. "Hop on while you can."

"Elizabeth!" I cupped my hands around my mouth. "Let's go."

She jogged down the hill. Her brown hair bounced with each step.

"You see anything?" I asked.

"Nope." Elizabeth panted. "No activity whatsoever."

"Good. Thanks for checking. Let's roll." I smiled.

The terrain was incredibly steep at times, and rocky at others. Some of the women held on for dear life just to stay on the mule. Never in my plan did I anticipate the hurdles we'd faced in the first day. What were the second or third day to bring?

The sun finally gave up, and darkness fell. We took it as a signal and stopped to set up for the night. We'd been moving for almost twenty-four hours; no matter what was behind us, we had to stop.

"Marsh." I walked over to him. "How's your arm?"

"It's not as bad as I thought." He stoked a small fire. Atop it was a large pot full of rice.

"Do you need some help?"

"Nah," he said. "Just check on the ladies."

I glanced over to the wood mule. They didn't need

checking on. Turned out the woman wasn't in labor. He knew it and so did I.

"Looks like they've got it under control," I said. "The canvas tent is a little small, but it'll cover most of us."

"Good." Marshall stirred the pot. "I can't believe we did it."

"Me neither." I kicked a rock. "Maybe we'll even get some sleep tonight."

"Here," he said, handing me a stack of flatbread. "Start handing this out. I'm afraid some will fall asleep before dinner. I don't want them to go to bed without something in their stomachs."

I took the soft bread from him and walked away. He wanted to be alone. It stung. I hoped he wasn't secretly cracking under the pressure.

Not like me.

CHAPTER 34

Since I was technically one of the pregnant women, I was one of the first to get a spot on the wagon to sleep under the canvas awning. We fit as many of the other women on as best we could, but still, some had to sleep underneath. I snuggled in my warm wool blanket, thankful I'd stolen Paul's secret stash and we weren't forced to use the body-odor-riddled ones in the jacks' tent.

Drifting to sleep was harder than I expected. Physically, I was exhausted, but I couldn't shut off my mind. What if Paul noticed we were gone sooner because I'd stolen his nice blankets? Could they have sobered up enough to try and track us last night?

A few people quietly sobbed, and then the weight of everything hit me. The pregnant women, formerly known as scrawn, were now given a chance at life along with their babies. With Paul, they faced certain death. But the others? What if I was getting them killed? Leading them to their deaths? I squeezed my eyes shut and pressed my palms over my ears, trying to quiet the thoughts.

Sleep finally took hold, but the nightmares returned. This time, Paul forced my hand to kill every woman and child. It felt so real. The weight of the cast-iron hand, the ax connecting with flesh. Worst of all was the warm blood spattering my face. I blinked myself awake. Why was my face wet?

It took a second to fully waken. Rain, not blood. The canvas was leaking. I buried my head under the blanket and cursed. Would we ever catch a break?

Sitting up hurt. A sharp ache burned deep in my fatigued back. But most of all, my calf seared with pain. I gingerly dangled my legs over the edge of the cart and nearly stepped on Frank.

"Sorry," I said.

He side-eyed me but said nothing. I guess he wasn't completely over my lie of omission. I was really becoming persona non grata lately.

Marshall came up to me and rested his arm on the edge of the wagon. "Is the canvas holding?"

"No," I said. "The rain woke me. Here"—I reached out my hand toward him—"get up here. It's not completely covered, but it's better than nothing."

"Hang on," Marshall said. "We've got to collect all our blankets and supplies before they're completely soaked."

"What time is it?" I jumped down and sidled up to Marshall. I couldn't deny it. He made me feel a way I hadn't in a long time.

"I'm guessing around four."

"Well," Frank announced. "I don't think we'll be getting any more sleep. We should trudge onward."

With all hands available, we loaded up in a matter of minutes while Marshall passed out a ration of berries.

"How's your burn?" I asked him.

"Not too bad." He shrugged.

I heaved a stack of wet blankets into a corner. "We'll need to dry those or they'll mildew."

Marshall tucked a non-existent strand of hair behind

my ear. "Let's not worry about that until it stops raining."

A shiver ran through my body. But not from the cold. *Stop it, Annalise.*

He stared at me for a moment, his hand lingering on the back of my neck.

"Guess we better get going." I turned as my heart fluttered.

Traveling in the rain was slow going. The heavy wheels slipped on the rocks and sunk in the mud. Frank did his best to maneuver the wood mule, but the task was slow and laborious. A squirrel ran next to us, much faster than we were moving. It felt like a pointed insult. I was soaked, couldn't get warm, and a harsh wind kicked up. My teeth chattered while I shivered. I avoided eye contact with the riders of the wagon. They were sedentary. I'm sure they were even colder than us.

Mud caked my boots, making them heavy as logs. Every step, they sunk in deeper and deeper. The black sky lifted to gray, so I assumed the sun was somewhere in the sky behind the thick clouds and relentless rain.

"How's everyone doing?" I yelled.

No one answered. Either they couldn't hear me over the rain, or were mad at me for dragging them into this. I guessed the latter.

So far, this was terrible. Everyone was exhausted, and I was pretty sure I heard someone sniffling. An illness would run through the camp quickly. I prayed it wasn't that.

Maybe certain death was our fate, and I had just prolonged it. Or sped it up, depending on the situation. I was fighting a plan that was bigger than me.

"Anna." Marshall snapped his fingers in front of my face. "Wake up."

"Sorry." I shook my head. "Why are we stopped?"

"No more dry wood," he said.

"Damn." I kicked at a muddy puddle. "This is all going to hell. Nothing has gone right. And now? Out of wood. We might as well lie down and die."

Marshall grabbed my shoulder and led me away into the timber. "Anna, you need to pull it together. Everyone is relying on us and Frank. If we crack, they crack."

"What's the point?" Frustrated tears streamed down my face. "We're doomed."

"Are you really giving up now?" he asked.

Ashamed, I fixed my gaze toward the ground.

"Look at us," he said. Arms splayed out, he spun in a circle. The rain had faded to a mist, but the cold still had a fierce bite. "We're free. Free of Paul. Free of the mechanicals. We choose our next step. We control our future. That is, unless you give up."

I wiped my tears with the sleeve of my wet flannel shirt. "Fine, Marsh, I'll put on a happy face, but I don't have a good feeling about any of this."

"It's all right." He walked toward me. He cupped the back of my neck and tilted my chin up at him. "Anna, I meant what I said before. I'm going to take care of you. Both of you. But I need you to be strong for a few more days, okay?"

I leaned in for a moment, but stopped myself. I didn't deserve him. "Sure, Marsh."

He held my gaze a moment longer and gently kissed my forehead.

"If you two are done playing grab ass over there, we could use your help," Frank said.

My cheeks warmed with embarrassment.

"I have an idea," Frank said.

CHAPTER 35

Chopping echoed through the thick, cold air. Everybody split wood, even the pregnant women.

"What are they doing?" I asked.

"They're getting to the center of the wood. It's dry. If we can get enough dry ones, we can start a fire and dry the rest of the wood around it."

"Brilliant."

"Are you guys hungry?" Marshall asked.

"I speak for everyone"—Frank motioned to the people behind him—"when I say yes, we are starving."

"How much longer until there's fire?" Marshall asked.

"It's hard to say," Frank said. "Did you pack any dried meats?"

"Yes." Marshall's eyes lit up. He ran over to his supplies and dug out a brown canvas bag. "Here." He handed us each a piece of pemmican. "I'll get some more flatbread too."

My stomach turned. Maybe my morning sickness was back. Pemmican didn't exactly make my list of favorite things to eat. I took a bite. The salty, rough texture fell apart in my mouth, and I washed it down with water.

I was startled by a loud crack of thunder, followed by another rainstorm. Everyone took cover and stacked the dry wood under the small, covered part of the canvas tent.

"Annalise." Hazel stalked toward me. "We can't start a fire in this rain!"

"And?" What did she want me to do about it?

"I'm cold, I'm hungry, and I'm sick of being wet," she said.

Why didn't she just punch me? I felt the same way, but Marsh was right. I couldn't crack, I had to show them if I was okay, they were okay. I had to put on a brave front.

"Are you sick of being alive?"

"What?" She backed up.

"Because if you're not," I said, "then stop complaining. So we had a bad day. Tomorrow might be better. It could be worse. But you and I both know this is a million times better than what's happening in Younish."

Her eyes welled with tears.

"Hazel," I said, pulling her into a tight hug. "I can't promise it's going to be okay. But I can promise that we have a chance."

"Fine." She pushed me away, crossed her arms, and rolled her eyes. A small tear escaped and streaked down her dirty cheek.

"One more thing." I leaned in and whispered, "Can you keep your whining to yourself? You're bringing down the entire group."

She turned and left in a huff. It made me laugh. She'd been a thorn in my side for the last two days. I basically told her what Marshall told me, but I wasn't as nice.

We all huddled for the rest of the afternoon. We didn't have enough wood to get far, so we opted to stay in place for the night. The rain finally stopped in the early evening, and we started a fire.

Everyone was miserable, cold, hungry, and in a bad mood by now. Lillian proudly stacked the cut dry wood and started the fire on her first try. We all clapped. Funny, we were cheering for heat; the simple fire brought us happiness. The brutes at Younish cheered when someone lost a limb to become a mechanical. Or when a mother was murdered . . . or her baby. I shuddered.

"Are you okay?" Marshall asked. He brushed past with a heavy kettle. He placed it on a rack over the fire. Flames lurched toward the dark sky.

"Yes," I said. "Just a little cold."

Marshall took bowls of chopped vegetables and placed them in the kettle. I wondered who was helping him. I felt like I was in a daze. Within an hour's time, I could smell a barley soup brewing. My stomach contracted.

Another kick? No, I think hunger. I needed to make myself useful, so I brought the wool blankets near the fire. I laid them out, hoping they'd dry faster.

Dinner was served, and no one spoke except for the occasional compliment to Marshall. We were weary and bone tired. I helped clean up and inspected the blankets. Many were dry, so I gave them to the pregnant women. Some were still sopping wet. I couldn't get them closer to the fire because the wood was the number one priority. It needed to be dry by the morning.

Frank's two friends were diligent about removing the dry wood to a covered part under the wagon and placing the wet pieces closer to the fire.

"It's fine." Marshall placed his hand on my shoulder from behind. "If we're short blankets, I'll volunteer first to do without."

"There are eight that are still wet. But sleeping-wise, we're only short one."

"Wow." Marshall laughed. "You actually stole every single one of Paul's blankets, didn't you?"

I shrugged. We walked over to the wagon. All spots were full. I'd be sleeping under the wagon tonight.

"I'm exhausted," I said. "Let's go to bed." I shuffled under the wagon and lay on my back. Marshall came in after but kept his distance. "Marsh? Come here."

He rolled over to me, on his side. I turned to my side facing him, throwing the blanket over both of us. He locked eyes with me.

"What? I don't want you to freeze." My smile faltered.

"It's going to be okay," Marshall said.

Burying my face in his chest, I cried quietly. I knew the people above me could hear despite my best attempts to stifle the crying. Marshall was warm and smelled like vegetable barley soup. He stroked my bald head and let me cry until I fell asleep.

I awoke for a moment to shift off my shoulder. Marshall was still holding me. For the first time in weeks, I felt safe, almost at peace.

CHAPTER 36

The morning sun had just started to light the sky, but it was still early and too dark to travel. I rolled onto my other side, my back now facing Marshall. He adjusted his grip and pulled me closer. Instinct or not, I liked it. I wanted him to hold me.

But it still felt like such a betrayal to Walter.

I squeezed my eyes shut and drifted to sleep. Just as I was about to fall into dreamland, a bellow turned my blood cold.

I'd heard that growl before.

A keringer.

My entire body froze with terror. I willed myself to roll over and face Marshall. He shifted; a small smile spread across his face as he awoke.

The beast bellowed again, but I couldn't pinpoint from which direction.

Marshall's eyes flew open.

I raised a finger to my lips.

"Anna, is that—" Marshall whispered.

"Yes." I motioned for him to move. "We have to get out of here. Can you get everyone up on the wagon? I need to find Frank."

"Yes." Marshall shimmied out from under the wagon. "We'll get the supplies loaded back on the wood mule."

I crawled out the underbelly of the wagon and sucked in a deep breath of the cold, humid morning air. The clouds of yesterday had finally broken, and the sky was a light purple. The sun would break the horizon completely soon and shine oranges and reds over us. I looked wildly around and didn't see the keringer, but that didn't mean it wasn't lurking behind a tree.

Frank was exiting the bottom of the wagon and I ran over to him. "Did you hear it?" I asked.

"Yes." He rubbed his hands over his face, shaking out the sleep. "A keringer. We knew it was only a matter of time before we saw one."

"We have to go. Marshall is waking everyone up and getting the mule reloaded with the supplies."

Just then, a flurry of confusion and chaos erupted from the wagon.

"A keringer!" someone screamed. "No!"

"Hurry!" a guy yelled, though I couldn't tell which one of Frank's friends said it.

The fear was palpable. I looked up. Marshall tried to keep everyone calm and quiet, but it was a lost cause. If the keringer wasn't positive of our location before, it was now.

Within ten minutes, we were loaded.

I pulled myself onto the wagon and stood near the throttle. "Everyone." I waved my hands to get their attention. Silence fell over them. It was an unnerving quiet. "We must leave immediately. Please, cram on as tightly as possible; it will be uncomfortable, but it'll be short term. We need volunteers to walk, maybe four or five." A few hands flew into the air. "Wait to hear the plan before you volunteer." I motioned for them to put their hands down. "I want the wagon at full speed. Race ahead and put as much distance between you and the keringer as you can. Head twenty miles north, set up camp, and we'll rendezvous tonight. The walkers will try to lead the keringer in another direction. There's a good chance whoever walks will have to fight off the keringer. If we don't make it to you by the morning, leave without us. We can't risk Paul catching up."

"I'll walk." Frank stood.

"Me too." Marshall stared at me.

Hazel slowly stood. "I'll walk."

"Great." Surprise colored my face. Hazel was the last person I expected to stay behind. "Let's see if everyone fits. Marshall, Hazel, can you grab some supplies for us to pack for the day?"

It became clear in a few moments that we needed an additional walker. The wagon was full, plus we needed the extra hands in case it came down to a battle.

One of Frank's friends jumped down, carrying an ax. Geez, I hadn't even bothered to learn his name. He was tall and strong. Paul would have classified him as a breeder. His blond hair was full and thick, but his baby face gave away his age. He couldn't have been older than me, twenty at the most.

"Thomas, my boy." Frank clapped him on the back.

"Tommy," he corrected him.

"Thank you, Tommy," I said. I needed to remember his name. I felt bad enough that I'd never bothered to introduce myself to him, and now I was indebted to him for his continued sacrifice.

"Off you go." I waved to the wagon. "We'll see you tonight. I hope."

The steam engine roared to life. A large woman with long blond hair stoked the fire, and it hobbled off into the rough forest terrain.

I turned to Hazel. "Thanks for walking with us."

She stared forward and said nothing. Her hands trembled. Without a word, we started after the wagon, keeping our eyes open and mouths shut. The wood mule was out of sight after the first hour. Two wheel marks, with crushed leaves and broken sticks, led the way.

It was easy to follow.

It would be easy for Paul to follow too.

"Hang on," Hazel said. She dropped her ax and pulled something from her pack. She twisted her long, curly hair into a bun at the nape of her neck. The loose tendrils gave it the appearance of a fancy updo. From the neck up, she looked as if she were going to a ball. "Did you guys hear that?"

I furrowed my brow. I hadn't heard anything. We all stopped and listened. A branch snapped nearby. That wasn't unusual, but this was a big snap, like a log. Then another broke.

We all scrambled together. With our backs facing each other, we formed a circle and surveyed the area.

"Remember," I whispered, "they can't see very good. Actually, at all, really. They spend most of their time in the dark. Worthless eyes mean they see by scent. Like a snake. If you're really in a jam, shed a piece of clothing and leave it on the ground. It'll get confused."

"She's right," Frank echoed. "And keep that as a last resort. Outrunning a keringer is nearly impossible."

"This keringer has been tracking us for the last hour," I said. "We need to kill it."

A loud snort echoed in the timber, followed by an ejection of mucus from its nose. Sweat dotted my brow. It was close.

We had three axes between us. Tommy and I held long, heavy sticks. I placed my stick on the ground, picked up a log, and threw it in the timber, hoping to draw out the beast.

It worked, a little too good.

CHAPTER 37

The keringer came rushing out behind a band of trees. Large, crepe-like, black wings told me it was male. He showed no fear as he careened directly at us. Stupidly, we scattered. Thirty seconds into the battle and he'd already outsmarted us. He was smaller, only five or six feet long, which was both good and bad. Good, because we might have a chance. Bad, because that meant he was a baby and his mother was most likely nearby.

Now, he was in the middle and we surrounded him. Our scent blanketed the area. I picked up another log and threw it at him. The beast swung around; his long tail whipped behind him. Marshall ducked just in time to avoid being stung by it.

"Come here, you big, ugly animal." I banged my stick on the ground and taunted him.

I nodded at Frank.

Frank gingerly stepped toward the keringer as I continued to slap the dirt. He lunged with his ax but missed. He pried the ax from the ground in a panic. The beast charged. Frank scrambled out of the away just in the nick of time. The keringer skidded to a stop and turned back toward us, puffing white fog out its nose.

Crap. We had to figure out a strategy. And fast.

The beast looked like a mangy bear with batwings

attached to it. He crawled around like an alligator on land. His tongue slithered in and out of his mouth like a lizard—tracking us. Using our individual scents to his benefit. His stalking stopped for a moment. The black tongue made a final appearance right before he charged Tommy.

I screamed and ran as hard as I could. I lifted the heavy stick over my head and slammed it into the keringer's side. His wing knocked me over. He whipped around, and I barely rolled out of the way. Tommy shrieked in pain.

"No!" I crawled toward Tommy and pulled him behind a bush. "Tommy, are you okay?"

"My arm. Its tail. It stung me." Tommy lifted his forearm. A defensive wound. "I'm okay." He clenched his jaw. His entire arm had already started to swell.

"Stay hidden back here," I said. "But stay alert, he might come back for you." I picked up Tommy's stick and ran back into the fray.

Hazel ran full force, sneaking up on the beast with her ax high above her head. She buried the ax deep into a haunch. The keringer thrashed and exposed his huge, sharp yellow fangs. Just like the one on Paul's mug.

She stepped back nimbly, but the keringer whipped around quickly with revenge and bit at her. His mouth opened and snapped shut over and over until he finally sunk his teeth into her shoulder. She screamed. Marshall threw a log at the beast to distract him.

The keringer turned, satisfied with his attack on Hazel, and licked the air toward Frank. Cords of saliva dripped from his fang tips. The beast paused for a moment and sprinted toward him. Frank pulled his ax up over his head. Ready to sacrifice himself for the chance to offer a killing blow to the beast.

"No!" I yelled.

Something came over me. It happened so fast. I picked up Hazel's fallen ax and sprinted. The hard ground slapped against my cold feet, but I felt like I was moving in slow motion. I jumped and landed on the beast's leathery skin just as he lunged at Frank. The keringer instinctively reared up on his hind legs but immediately faltered. The wound Hazel had caused the beast may have just saved both my and Frank's life.

The beast flailed from side to side, trying buck me off. I gripped him with my thighs, lifted my weapon over my head, and swung. The heavy ax lodged itself deep into the top of the keringer's head. Blood spurted along the edges of the blade. I yanked it from his head. Blood flowed out like a water fountain. He kicked wildly, so I jumped off. I rolled out of the beast's way as he staggered before falling on his side. A pool of crimson liquid soaked into the ground surrounding him.

I stared with my mouth agape and my breath coming in short spurts. My chest heaved.

"Frank," I said. "Are you okay?"

He was already up and running to Hazel's side. She was in shock; her face was white as fresh snow. Her eyes stared forward but looked vacant, and she gripped her shoulder.

"Hazel." Frank snapped his fingers in front of her face.

She blinked and shook her head. "Am I going to die?'

He pulled her hand away and examined the shoulder. "Die?" He stifled a laugh.

"Hazel—" He grabbed his side and laughed.

He'd either snapped or lost his mind. I squatted and pushed his hand away to examine her myself. "Oh, Hazel," I said. "It barely broke the skin."

"What?" she asked. "But I thought he bit me!"

"You must have been quicker than you thought." I pulled her shirt back over her shoulder. "I'm not even sure this wound needs cleaning. Guess you need to thank your lucky stars."

"I guess so," she said absently.

Marshall had been tending to Tommy this whole time.

"How bad is it?" I asked.

"I said I'm okay," Tommy said.

He wasn't.

"His whole arm is incredibly swollen." Marshall turned toward us. "I'm not sure what to do. Any ideas?"

I shook my head.

"Keep it elevated." Frank picked up a stick. "I think we need to splint it too."

He ripped part of his flannel shirt and shredded it into five pieces. Then he placed the stick flush with Tommy's arm and used the strips to tie it in place. Tommy still seemed stunned but never complained.

I gathered up his pack and combined it with mine. It would be heavy, but we needed the supplies. I looked up at the hill to regain my bearings, and saw the threat we'd ignored.

The keringer's mother stood high above us. Her silhouette dotted the top of the ridge.

"Guys." My voice trembled. "We need to get out of here now. Tommy, can you run?"

He nodded.

"I don't know if I can," Hazel said. "I'm still so dizzy."

"Well, you're going to need to suck it up." I glanced over at the ridge again. "That keringer was a baby."

"A baby!" Hazel yelled.

"Yes." I pointed. "His mom is right up there. And she's pissed. We need to lose her."

"Follow me." Frank looked over his shoulder once more before he ran.

What had we done?

CHAPTER 38

Between the five of us, we had one bum leg, a burned arm, a grazed shoulder, and a nearly useless arm. What a bunch. But we ran, zigzagging through the timber, depositing our scent as we went, hoping to confuse the mother keringer. When we stopped for a quick break, the men relieved themselves in all different directions. They marked the area like dogs. Hopefully, it would further throw off our scent.

We pushed forward. My stomach growled, but I said nothing. I looked to Tommy. His face never showed any pain, but I wondered how he was running with an arm that looked like it was going to burst through the skin. I imagined the throbbing was horrific.

The timber grew thinner, and I had a hard time keeping track of the wagon trail. The tracks were lighter. A hard wind had dried out the topsoil and blown fresh dirt over the tracks.

Along the horizon was a scene my brain couldn't make sense of. It looked like some large contraption sticking straight into the sky.

"What the . . ." Tommy trailed off. "Does anyone else see what I'm seeing or am I hallucinating?" He pointed with his stiff, swollen, splinted arm. It would have been comical if it hadn't been so sad.

"Is that . . . what is that?" I asked. Thankful for the break, I rested my hands on my knees and caught my breath.

"Hang on." Marshall climbed up a branch on a nearby tree, then another. "I was slated to be a whistle punk until my position was switched last minute."

Marshall had been my friend for years, but I'd never known that he wanted to be a whistle punk, and I'd certainly never seen him climb a tree before. Even with his burned arm, he still climbed like a pro. He finally settled on a branch and stared from his vantage point. Almost as quickly as he climbed, he descended. But there was something about his quickness that gave me pause. He seemed panicked.

"What is it?" I asked. "Is everything all right?"

"No." Marshall was panting. "That's our wood mule. It's crashed! I think it ran into a keringer pit."

"Oh, no." My heart dropped into my stomach.

I took off running and everyone followed suit. Tears filled my eyes, and only the speed from my run kept them at bay.

As I got closer, I understood exactly what had happened. They must have been going too fast, or the lookout got lazy. My worst fears were confirmed: They'd wrecked into a keringer pit. The nose of the mule was deep in the pit, and the back was vertical, like a capsized boat before it sank.

"Annalise," Lillian yelled. "Thank goodness you're back." She embraced me.

"What happened?" I asked.

"We didn't see it. It was covered in leaves and pine needles."

I watched Marshall run past me and directly in front of the huge pit. He dropped to his knees and rested his face in his hands. "What aren't you telling me?" I said carefully.

"It's Elizabeth." Lillian broke into sobs. "She fell off the end when we hit the pit. She fell in."

"She. Fell. In."

Lillian nodded and continued to cry.

"Well," Hazel said, putting her hands on her hips, "I got bitten by a keringer, if anyone cares."

"Not now, Hazel! Has anyone gone down to get her?" I yelled. "Why? Why is this happening?" My chest felt heavy, and my voice cracked as I shrieked. "How much more can we take?" I screamed until my throat was raw. "Is this our fate? Are we meant to die out here?" I screamed between sobs. My voice echoed.

"Annalise!" Frank said. "Keep it down! You'll alert the keringer! Or worse—Paul."

I felt a hand gently touch my shoulder. Then another, and another. I didn't look up; I was too broken, too ashamed.

"Annalise," Frank said.

I glanced at his face. He looked as if he was searching for the right words.

"Anna," Marshall said. "I wish you could see yourself the way I see you. The way we all see you." One by one, they all murmured in agreeance. "You've been carrying this burden for us. In reality, we'd all be dead within the year. You gave us this chance at a better life. Heck, you gave us a chance at life. Which is more than we had at Younish." He tilted my chin up so I was forced to look at his face. "You saved us. Now let us save you."

Lillian knelt next to me. "Let's just sit and collect our thoughts while they get the mule dislodged from the pit, okay? Then they can get Elizabeth out."

She pulled me into her embrace, and I rested my head

on her shoulder. Despite the last few days of travel, she still smelled sweet, like honey. The gravity of it all hit me harder than I ever imagined.

I sat and stared blankly until it was early afternoon. I heard footsteps approaching. Frank's exhausted voice brought me back to reality. "We got it out. Elizabeth is still down there, and she's alive. Or she was."

"How do you know?" I wiped my nose with the back of my shirt and stood.

"We could hear her crying," Frank said.

"I'm going down there to get her."

CHAPTER 39

To say a keringer pit looked like the ground swallowed itself would be an exact and accurate description. No one actually knew how one was made, or if they did, they weren't alive to tell the story.

"Annalise." Frank stepped toward me. "I'll go down."

"No." I stood firmly. I had to do this. Falling apart in front of the entire group should have left me embarrassed. But everyone rallied around me. They believed in me. If they believed in me, I needed to believe in myself. "I brought her out here. I need to rescue her."

"But . . . you . . ." Frank stammered. "You know, your *situation*."

"Even with my *situation* . . ." I rolled my eyes. "I'm still more agile than you."

"I wouldn't argue with her when she's like this," Marshall said. "It's a never ending battle. I'll grab the rope."

"Marshall's right," I said. "This is my mess. I need to fix it."

I hadn't even thought about my baby in this equation. The morning sickness had mostly subsided, and my energy was back to normal. Compared to how I'd felt a few days ago, I was doing great.

A rope slipped around me, just below my bust. I turned and locked eyes with Marshall.

"Is this okay?" he asked. "It's not squishing the baby, is it?"

"No." I winced. "It's a little awkward to put the rope here, but it'll be fine."

I peered over the lip and tried to gauge the depth of the pit. My stomach dropped. Somehow, I'd forgotten about my fear of heights until now. The bottom was certainly there. I just couldn't see it. Densely packed trees pointing at odd directions blocked my view. They were growing out the sides, up toward the sun. It looked like someone staked them in at an angle.

I sat dangling my feet over the edge, leaning forward for a better vantage point. Nearly ten feet down, a jagged trunk showed fresh marks of trauma. It looked like maybe Elizabeth had fallen on the tree, and it snapped, then carved a path for her body on its descent.

I shuddered.

Marshall sat next to me. "Are you ready?"

"Yes." I turned. They'd rolled a heavy, downed tree to the side to use as leverage as they lowered me. My luck, I'd pull them all down behind me. Thankfully, they were better planners than me.

I shimmied down the edge until my feet were firmly on a tree. My shaky hands gripped the bark below, and I swung my feet down until I reached another branch.

"More slack!" I yelled.

With a loose rope, I repeated this action over and over. My tummy was in the way, and I kept kneeing myself in the stomach. The light waned, and I'd only descended maybe fifteen feet.

The lower I progressed, the more horizontal the trees grew. A clear path on the left side of the pit revealed Elizabeth's fall. Broken trees and branches, clumps of brown hair and streaks of blood were her breadcrumb trail. I swallowed hard.

My breath was heavy, and my clothes were sticky with pine sap. I sat on a thick branch to rest.

"How are you, Anna?" Marshall's voice echoed down.

I flinched and wiped the sweat off my brow with my sleeve. "Peachy."

My feet fluttered below me to gain purchase on another branch. But nothing was there.

"Marsh," I yelled, "I need more slack."

"More?" he asked. "We're out of rope."

"Okay," I said. "Well, I've got at least ten more feet to drop. I'm going to untie myself and go down the rest of the way without it. Can you figure out how to make a longer rope so I can get back up?"

"Yes," his voice echoed. "If you wait a little bit, we can add to the rope and lower you down."

"No," I said. "We don't have that kind of time to waste. The keringer could return any minute. I've got this."

Untying my lifeline proved to be difficult. First, it was a tight knot that only got tighter as I'd put tension on the rope. Then, the branches scratched my arms. And lastly, I was afraid. If I fell and hurt myself, I'd be no help to Elizabeth. Worse, what if I hurt my baby? I shook my head. There was no turning back now.

The coarse rope finally budged. I let out a deep breath and rubbed my sore ribs. The sun from above cast a sliver of light through the trees.

I shimmied out toward the edge of the branch until it started to bow downward. Dropping my hands down, I gripped it and, hand over hand, made my way to the edge. It bent and I pointed my toes, hoping they'd reach a branch thick enough to support my weight. The skin on my palms was starting to rip.

The tips of my toes brushed against a flimsy branch. The pine needles tickled my legs. My grip slipped and I fell. Hitting the thin branches wasn't that bad; the foliage on them hurt worse than the actual wood. The small branches were quickly replaced with full, thick ones. I waved my arms and eventually caught myself between two. I let out a small cry. Assessing my injuries would have to wait. I needed to keep moving. I was now in a grove of trees growing from the ground up. I heard moaning from below. I was close.

Maybe I should have let Marshall do this. He was trained to be a whistle punk, after all. I was regretting my decision. Why was I so impulsive? I'd gotten myself into so much trouble over the last week with my rash decisions.

Deep in thought and scolding myself, I didn't realize I'd made it all the way down until my foot hit the solid earth. I looked up. The tree that had cut out Elizabeth's fall allowed some, but not a lot, of light to cast into the pit.

Piles of bones were scattered along the walls. Deer, elk, and bear bones were licked clean. The pit still reeked of death. I tripped over something attached to a large bone. My hands caught me just in time.

It was a pair of canvas pants. A human femur poked out of the bottom of them.

CHAPTER 40

I jumped to my feet and stared into the corner. There was a collection of at least ten human skulls. If I stayed down here much longer, there would be twelve. Either this was a very prolific keringer, or she was one that didn't move around often.

I heard sniffling before I saw it. My curiosity of the pit was now on the backburner. A chill ran down my spine and I shivered.

"Elizabeth?" I whispered. "Is that you?"

I ran to her. There was no answer. She was unconscious but still moaned in pain and was completely hidden in the shadows amongst the dried bones. If not for her weak cries, I wouldn't have found her so quickly. I placed my forearms under her armpits and pulled her out into the column of light from above. A two-inch chunk of hair and scalp was missing. She was covered in cuts and scrapes, and one eye was black and blue. I sucked in a sharp breath. Worst of all, her right leg was twisted in an unnatural angle. She started to stir.

After a few moans, her eyes fluttered open. "Annalise?" she cried.

"It's okay." I held her head. "You're going to be okay."

"What happened?"

She was crying so hard, I had a difficult time understanding her. She mumbled inaudible sentences. I ripped a piece of my shirt off and pressed it to her scalp to stop the bleeding. "The wagon crashed. You fell into a keringer pit. It looks like a tree took most of the impact for you, but you're still injured."

"Am I—" She sobbed. "Am I going to die?"

"No," I said firmly. "Not today. Wait here." I cringed, and ran to the main opening. "Marshall," I yelled. "Drop down more rope. I found Elizabeth."

"Stand back," Marshall yelled in return. "Is she all right?"

I stood back and heard the heavy rope fall in the newly-created opening, courtesy of Elizabeth and the tree.

"She's got a broken leg and some lacerations, but she'll survive. We need to get out of here."

Adrenaline had worn off and panic had set in. The realization of being in the bottom of a huge keringer pit hit me hard. I ran over to Elizabeth and tripped again on a bone. This time, I didn't look to see if it was human.

"Do you want me to drag you over there?" I asked. "Or would you like to try to walk on your good leg?"

"Walk," she said.

I hoisted her up. She cried out in pain.

"I don't think I can," she said. "Leave me here, I'll only slow you down."

"Come on," I grunted. "You can do this, Elizabeth. Do not give up on me now. Besides, just think of all the fun campfire stories you'll be telling a year from now."

She tried to laugh.

"You'll be a hero," I said. "I don't know a lot of people who have fallen into a keringer pit and survived."

"We haven't survived yet."

She had a point. But today wasn't going to be my last.

We made it to the grove of trees in the center. I propped her up and ran to the rope. I reached for it, but it was abruptly pulled up.

"Hey!" I yelled. "I wasn't ready, send it back down."

Silence.

A crack as loud as thunder boomed through the pit. A thick tree came careening toward us, demolishing all branches and horizontally growing pines covering the pit. I yanked Elizabeth to safety. A waterfall of logs, dirt, and leaves rained into the pit.

Yelling and chaos ensued above.

We were trapped.

CHAPTER 41

Faint screams echoed above. Elizabeth sobbed, her face etched with fear. I paced back and forth until I thought I'd go mad.

I needed to know what was happening up there. Had Paul found us? Or another crew? I had to get us out of here. We were sitting ducks.

"Elizabeth." I knelt next to her. "I'm going to see what's in that direction. Maybe there's another way out."

"No." She leaned her head back onto the rough bark of a tree, then winced and shifted her broken leg. "Don't leave me."

"I have to," I said. "Besides, I should probably splint your leg. I'll be back." I squeezed her hands. "I promise."

She abruptly pulled her hands back and looked away. The journey into the cavern wasn't far. I walked roughly fifty feet. My heart pounded in my chest. I ground my teeth and pressed forward.

My foot slipped on the wet dirt, so I stopped. I questioned my decision to explore the cave. Behind me, the light was almost completely gone. In front of me, maybe one hundred yards or more, was a sliver of light that beckoned me forward. It was like being stuck in the middle of a tunnel.

I looked forward and back again. The darkness disoriented me. I crouched down and gathered my thoughts. Something echoed to my left. My hands shook. Despite the cold, sweat dotted my brow. I jumped and ran—no sprinted—back toward Elizabeth. As the light drew near, I tried to slow myself.

"Annalise!"

"Elizabeth." I breathed a sigh of relief. "I told you I'd come back."

"Did you find something for my leg?" she asked.

I scanned the area and walked up to a tree. "Yes." I snapped off the branch and used my pocketknife to clear any small twigs and needles. I'd truly become quite the knot bumper.

I laid the branch next to her leg and studied Elizabeth's face. Her fear of being left behind turned to fear of pain. I took the wrap off her head and ripped the rest of my sleeve and shredded it into strips.

"Elizabeth," I said carefully. "I need you to be quiet. This is going to be the worst pain you've ever felt. But if you scream, whatever is happening above will be coming for us next. And if it's Paul, you know he'll make us suffer."

She reached over and grabbed a piece of bark. "Let's get this over with."

She gritted the wood between her teeth.

The upper portion of her leg was uninjured. Swollen, but uninjured. I started there and stabilized her thigh first. Once I got to her knee, I knew it was going to get dicey. I secured a strip of cloth under her leg.

"Okay." I lifted each side of the cloth. "Bite down on three. One, two, three." In a swift motion, I knotted the strip to her knee. Her tibia shifted as I tightened the cloth.

Elizabeth groaned and cried.

My stomach constricted, and I fought the urge to barf.

"I'm sorry, I have to do another one," I said. "Again, one, two, three." I repeated this until I was down to her ankle. The bones naturally wanted to shift back into place. She breathed heavily and her eyes fluttered. She was on the brink of passing out again. I was satisfied with the splint job. Her leg was straight, and it seemed like the bones were aligned. I wasn't a doctor, but it would have to do for now.

Elizabeth's face was slick with sweat. Her bloody cheeks had clear tracks from tears, and her face twisted in pain and fatigue. Her energy stores were zapped. I wished I had some water or food to offer her.

Branches from above cracked at an alarming rate. Pine needles and leaves spilled down. It felt like I was watching it in slow motion. A huge shadow was getting larger and larger as it readied to collide with the earth. I cursed. I grabbed Elizabeth under her arms and pulled her even farther away from the opening.

A small earthquake shook the pit floor. A plume of dust particles settled and exposed what fell from our escape route. The beast groaned. It struggled to its feet.

A keringer.

The mother keringer had tracked us down.

CHAPTER 42

If someone would have told me I'd encounter a keringer twice in one day, I would have assumed it was because I died twice. I never thought it'd be like this.

The mother keringer staggered a few steps and fell. Her heavy, musky, and warm breath kicked up dust. My hands shook, but I still approached the beast. I locked eyes with her. She was bleeding, and her back appeared to be broken. She cried out in pain.

I prayed everyone above was okay. But something took me in that moment. She was a mother. We'd killed her baby. He had attacked us, and it was a kill or be killed situation. But still, she'd seen her baby expire before her eyes, and she wanted revenge. Any mother would do the same.

I know I would.

A pit formed in my stomach. I pulled my knife from my belt. My entire body tremored as I got within arm's distance of her. Her eyes tracked me, but she didn't move. I placed my hand on the top of her sweaty head.

"I'm sorry," I whispered to her.

She stared back at me, as if she understood.

I plunged my knife deep into her neck and pulled back when I hit a bone. She bellowed deeply, never taking her eyes off me. Blood spurted on my belly, and a large puddle quickly formed. She released a deep breath. A breath of relief. And then nothing. I had put her out of her misery. Comfort wasn't something I could offer her, but a quick death was. We owed her that much.

Something hit me in the back of the neck. I grabbed at it wildly.

The rope. It was back.

"Elizabeth." I placed my hands under her arms and lifted her to her feet. "We have to go." I wiped my bloodied hands on my pants.

"Are you okay?" A voice echoed down at us.

"Yes," I yelled back. "A warning would have been nice. Is everyone okay up there?"

No one answered.

Elizabeth was in rough shape, but she had to hold on for a little longer. Just until we could get her on the mule, then she could rest. I tied the rope into a giant noose. She stood on one leg and I placed the rope under her butt. I took each of her hands and placed them firmly on each side of the rope.

"When they pull"—I motioned up—"let your legs come up. Pretend you are on a swing. Hold on as tight as you can."

She nodded. Her breath was ragged.

I held her chin. "Elizabeth, you are strong. You come from a line of celebrated lumberjacks."

"But I'm a scrawn." Her eyes darted to the ground.

"Stop it!" I yelled. "No, you're not. No one is a scrawn or a breeder. We're just men and women. Smart ones, I might add." We didn't have time for this. I hoped she was ready. "Now hold on." I jerked the rope twice, and it slowly ascended.

With Elizabeth headed to safety, I walked to the keringer. My boot slipped on the large puddle of blood.

The opportunity to gain a closer look at her was gnawing at me. I'd never been this close to one before, so I hadn't noticed the subtle black and brown stripes in between patches of coarse hair. I rubbed my fingertips up and down on the hairless parts, studying the stripes. If there was a pattern, I couldn't figure it out. Her face was small, with a flat nose. Two exposed saber teeth were on either side of her mouth. I examined the fangs, slowly lifting the lips on each side of the muzzle.

The fangs curved just like the handle on Paul's ale mug.

I rubbed my hand over her face. "Thank you," I whispered to her.

With my sharp knife, I dug around the circumference of her gums. The tooth came loose after a few hearty tugs. The root extended to six inches. I wiped the bloody tooth on my pant leg, and I placed it in my back pocket.

"Anna," a voice yelled down. "Where are you? Let's go."

I shook my head. I wondered how long they'd been waiting for me. Now it was my turn to sit in the swing.

Even with my hands gripping the rope tightly, I couldn't relax while they brought me up. But I still closed my eyes and did my best. What else could go wrong? I laughed. Bad things come in threes, I'd always heard. Surely, we'd hit that quota.

Frantic movement and conversation broke my trance. My eyes whipped open. I was near the top. Frank had his arms out, and he tugged at me before I had the chance to pull myself off.

"No!" I sucked in a sharp breath. Two lifeless bodies lay near the edge. One was so mangled, I didn't know who it was. The other was the lumberjack Frank had brought along. Brad. And now he was just gone. Poof. A life greased out.

Tommy sat next to a tree, his splint either removed or yanked off, crying. His knees were up to his chest. The palms of his hands pressed into his eyes.

What used to be a wood mule was on its side. Two wheels were a pile of splinters, and thick, black oil leaked out the side of the engine.

Marshall.

"Frank!" I scanned the area frantically. "Where is Marshall?" I didn't wait for an answer. I ran. "Marshall. Marshall!" My voice cracked.

On the other side of the wood mule, I found him slumped against the overturned wagon. His glassy-eyed gaze was forward and unfocused. I rushed to his side and knelt beside him.

"Marsh?" My shaking hand gently touched a cut above his eyebrow. I examined him. He didn't appear to be injured anywhere else, but he was shaken. "Look at me. What happened?"

"She came for us." He stared forward. His voice was flat, devoid of emotion. "The mother keringer. I suppose it was only a matter of time, like Frank said. She tracked us."

Frank had a gash in the back of his shirt, and blood rimmed it. Hazel limped. Lillian lay on her back amongst the shredded canvas tent. Her heaving chest was the only indication she was alive. Every single one of us was injured in one way or another. The keringer had hurt us. Revenge for her baby. I shook my head.

"Marsh." I gently turned his face. "Are you hurt?"

"No." He finally locked eyes with me.

"Who?" I pointed. "Who did we lose?"

"Brad." Marshall broke down and sobbed. He covered his eyes with a hand. "And Dorothy."

"No," I whispered.

Dorothy had been tall and heavy—everything Paul was looking for in women. She would have had a chance at life in Younish if I hadn't convinced her to come out here with us. She wasn't destined for death; she was destined to bring life into this world, even though it would be under the rule of my brother. Yet, here she was. I had walked her to the edge of freedom, given her a semblance of autonomy, and let her die.

I stood abruptly. We had to get out of here. I frantically gathered up the blankets. Tying one blanket to a large stick, I created a pouch to store our supplies. I did the same on the other side of the stick and brought it to Frank.

"Here." I handed it to him. "Can you replicate this? The heavily pregnant may not be able to carry anything at all, but the rest of us can pick up their slack."

"Annalise," Frank said. "Do you think we should set up camp for the night? We're all pretty shaken from the attack."

"No!" I stood close to him. "The longer we stay around the destruction, the worse morale is going to become. Plus, Paul could be right on our heels."

He held his chin thoughtfully. "We need to at least bury our dead."

"Of course." I nodded. "Try out this pack."

He bent at the knees and put the heavy wood between his shoulder blades. It extended four inches past each shoulder, and the bags hung limply.

"I think this might work." He rested his palms on the sticks on either side of his shoulders.

"Fine." I handed him the rest of the blankets. "I'll dig

the graves with Marshall, and you can direct the rest to create packs like these and gather all they can carry."

I turned and walked back to Marshall. "Can you stand now?" I asked. "We need to bury Brad and Dorothy."

He slowly stood. The ground tremored slightly with his heavy footsteps behind me. We only had two small shovels, but we made do. Marshall avoided all eye contact. Digging in silence was horribly awkward. Marshall always had the right words for me, and here he was, in deep distress, and I had nothing for him. He deserved better.

"Done," Frank said.

"Okay." I whipped around. "Elizabeth's leg is broken. I splinted it. But I think we're going to need to make a stretcher."

"We're out of blankets, so we can't use those," he said. "What do you think?"

"I don't know," I snapped. My shovel hit the dirt, and I rubbed my hands over my head. "I'm sorry. I just . . . I don't have the answers."

"It's fine." Frank held his hands out. "We'll figure something out."

"I think we're ready for them," I said. "Dorothy and Brad."

Marshall still said nothing, but walked over to Brad. He picked up his hands, and I grabbed his bloody legs. His dungarees were saturated in blood and squished in my hands. The air was thick with a copper scent. His heavy body bowed as we carried him to the grave.

People started gathering around us. I had to get Dorothy in the ground before they saw her gruesome injuries.

"Marsh." I tugged on his shoulder. He turned. I

nodded my head toward Dorothy's lifeless body. "I don't want them to see."

His answer was a deep breath and a nod.

I picked up her cold arms. Her head had been smashed several times by the beast. Her obliterated jaw had been ripped free from her head. The ridged windpipe was exposed, filleted into pink ribbons. Her neck hung limply as we carried her to the shallow grave. The moment she was in, I quickly placed dirt over her.

The remaining nineteen of us gathered around in a circle and stared at the shallow graves. Frank spoke, but I doubt anyone heard the words. We were all stunned, frightened, and tired. Oddly, no one cried. Maybe they were out of tears, but the melancholy was overwhelming. At least to me.

This had to end.

I backed up to a pack and knelt until it was firmly on either side of my shoulders and stood. The weight of it was more than I expected, but we couldn't leave our precious supplies behind. With the wood mule completely obliterated, this was our only choice.

"We'll head up over that mountain pass." Frank pointed.

I'd never gone over a mountain before. It didn't look very far away. In fact, we were already in the foothills. But nothing about this trip had been easy. I wouldn't underestimate the terrain.

"If we make it to the base of the saddle, we can set up camp for the night." He pointed to the low spot between two peaks.

"What about Elizabeth?" I asked.

"You should have just left me in that pit," she said. Her eyes were rimmed red. "I'll only slow you down."

"Elizabeth." I crouched next to her, careful not to

touch her leg. "You're coming with us. Your life is valuable." She broke my eye contact. I held her chin and forced her to look at me. "*All* our lives are valuable. We've lost two in that fight. We can't—no, we *won't*—lose anyone else."

"She's right," Frank echoed. "We've made you a stretcher. It'll take us up to the base tonight. We'll have to figure out something else for tomorrow. But let's deal with this for now."

The stretcher was two branches and canvas strung between them. Marshall picked up one end, and Frank the other. The seven bigger and stronger women also took turns carrying Elizabeth and supplies. A few of the smaller women who weren't pregnant helped, but they couldn't carry her for very long.

It felt like we walked vertically for miles. Sometimes, it was so steep I feared I'd fall backward. Evening was upon us. Above the tree line, the terrain turned rockier. With the sun set and the moon shining through the clouded night skies, we stopped our journey just before the peak. A few patches of drifted snow scattered the barren landscape. I hated being above the tree line. There was no cover, and all we had for shelter were piles of boulders.

"Is this far enough?" I asked Frank.

"I suppose so. We better get a fire going before it gets too cold."

Too cold? It was freezing. And humid. There was nothing worse than a wet cold. We sidled up against a few boulders. It would be a long night. Marshall placed a pot on the roaring fire. His comfort zone. I guessed he was cooking to mentally escape the last day.

"Hey," I said to him. "Smells good."

"It's vegetable barley soup again," he said.

"Good. That was delicious." I plopped on the frozen ground next to him. "Marsh, are you okay?"

He finally looked at me. "Anna, I could have died."

"But you didn't."

"I promised," he interrupted. "I promised to take care of you and the baby. You've been through enough. Let down too many times. I almost let you down. In the most permanent way possible."

"Are you crazy? That's what got you so bothered? I thought you were traumatized." I laughed. "Marsh, we have to take this day by day. Heck, minute by minute. I'm not your responsibility. You've already done so much."

He stared at me with sadness in his eyes. I wanted to make him feel better, but I didn't have the words. Truth was, I'd already lost Walter, and I didn't know what I'd do if I lost him too.

"Please, Marsh," I said. "I need you to be the strong one. I'm the reckless one, you're the voice of reason. That's just how it is."

A lopsided grin formed on his lips. "I'll try."

"I mean it, Marsh." I rested my hand on my stomach. "Do it for . . ." I hesitated. "Just do it for all of us. Okay?"

He stared at the swirling liquid in the pot, never looking in my direction, and nodded.

We all gathered around and ate. The conversation was awkward and forced. Tommy's arm wasn't swollen anymore. Whatever poison the keringer's tail injected into him had worn off. He said it was stiff, but better. Elizabeth wasn't faring as well as I'd hoped. She did her best to steady her breathing, but the pain was winning, and she'd cry out if she moved even in the slightest.

I was worried infection would set in, but I had no formal training. I didn't know how to even check for it.

Hazel went on and on about her tiny bite on her shoulder and how she nearly broke her ankle slipping on wet pine needles when she jumped out of the way. She was overly dramatic, so I ignored her.

Tomorrow was going to present a whole new set of challenges. But for now, I needed to sleep.

Once dinner was cleaned up, we did our best to make ourselves comfortable. I leaned against a rock, but it was so cold, it sucked the heat right out of my back. Marshall sat stretching his neck from side to side. Instead of asking and putting him on the spot, I simply sat behind him and rested my back against his. It was too cold to lie down; sitting back to back was the next best thing.

"Thanks, Marsh," I said. I wrapped a blanket around myself.

"Are you comfy?" he asked.

I fell asleep before I could answer.

CHAPTER 43

Waking on your own because your body and mind are well rested is a great feeling. Needless to say, that's not why I awoke that dark morning. My teeth chattered so hard, I thought they'd shatter. My entire body tremored, and my breath hung in the air, nearly frozen the second I exhaled. The heavy wool blanket was no match for the subzero mountain temperature.

Stretching my stiff body, I felt Marshall stir behind me. I stood, and pins and needles shot up my sore feet. The air was so cold, it stung my eyes.

"Anna," Marshall said. "How are you?"

"Just cold." I wrapped the blanket over my shoulders. He stood and walked toward me. He pulled a piece of twine from his back pocket. "Here, let me tie this around your waist. We'll make ponchos out of a few blankets."

"What about the supplies?" I asked.

"We emptied one blanket last night." He gently tied the twine around me. "We'll empty another this morning. In fact, I need to hand out dried meat and bread."

"That's two," I protested. "That leaves seventeen people without a blanket."

"We'll just have to make do," Frank interrupted. "Marshall, fine idea about getting breakfast out." Marshall walked away. "Annalise, we can't carry Elizabeth today on the gurney. It's too rugged."

"I know." I looked down.

"We can use the canvas from the gurney to make bags for supplies, maybe free up four or five blankets." He stroked his beard. "We'll take turns with the ponchos."

"What about Elizabeth?" I lowered my voice.

"We'll have to act as a crutch, I guess," he said. "Elizabeth." His voice cut through the icy air like a knife.

"Hmm?" she replied. Her voice was groggy and thick.

"How are you feeling this morning?"

"I feel like I have a broken leg," she said. "How are you feeling? Like you have red hair? Yes?"

Frank's brow knitted in confusion.

"Any other obvious observations you'd like me to make?" she asked.

I rushed over and squatted next to her, the frozen ground as hard as granite against my feet. "Elizabeth, can you walk if we help?"

"I don't have much of a choice, do I?"

"No." I shook my head. "Not really. Make sure you get some breakfast."

She nodded. Her voice was thick with sarcasm, but fear was etched on her face. I told myself we wouldn't leave her behind, but I wasn't sure I'd keep that promise.

We were able to make six packs out of the canvas strips from the gurney. With eight blankets in total, that still left nine people without. Even with my makeshift poncho, I was still cold. High winds ripped right through my clothes. The humid air bit at my skin and managed to soak through my boots. It was lightly snowing, and it only added to my misery. I hoped the sun would crest soon.

The higher we climbed, the rockier the terrain became.

Initially, we could walk around the larger jutting rocks. But after an hour it became evident we'd need to climb on top of them. As the sun made its ascent, the clouds fought for the spotlight. We'd only be getting a gray sky today.

Jagged, black rocks filled the mountain landscape. It was a constant battle of finding the right foothold, leading Elizabeth, and not slipping on the slick stones. A gasp followed by frantic steps or a fall became our marching song. It was ironic considering the jacks would sing songs to pass the time. I took a step and lifted my sore leg; it was caught in between two rocks. My momentum was already forward, and I couldn't free myself from the fall. I cursed as I braced myself. Pain shot up my right hand.

"Anna!" Marshall rushed to my side.

"I'm fine." I grunted, and turned my body halfway over, trying to get a look at my wedged foot. "I'm stuck."

Marshall pulled on the smaller of the two rocks, freeing me. I brought my hand up to my eyes. Crimson blood flowed down my palm through my ripped glove.

"Well, this sucks." My hand was already cold—now it was raw, wet, and cold. Perfect. I looked at Elizabeth and quieted. All things considered, it could be worse.

The air became thinner, and my chest heaved. I was having a hard time catching my breath in the altitude, so I stopped for a moment and watched Marshall. Elizabeth's arm was draped over his shoulder. His other arm was wrapped around her waist as he guided her through the terrain. He took special care to lift her so her broken leg never touched the ground. I could see why she preferred his help over mine.

I decided staring directly at the ground made it feel like I wasn't traveling straight up a mountain pass, so I focused on that. It felt liked we'd been traveling for hours, and we still hadn't crested the mountain.

"This is as good a place as any," Frank said, breaking the silence. "Let's eat." He looked at the sky, reading the sun. "It's after lunch anyway. We need a break."

"I don't want to stop for too long," I said. "The less we move, the colder we'll get."

"True," Hazel said. She hadn't spoken to me in a while. I was thankful for that.

"Then no hot lunch," Frank said.

Several people groaned. I was just as sick of the flatbread and pemmican as everyone else, but we had to keep moving. I sat on a flat rock, ripped a piece of bread with my teeth, and chewed. I didn't realize how thirsty I was until that moment. Not wanting to be a bother, I picked up a hunk of snow and let it melt in my mouth. Big mistake. My body chilled from the inside out.

I exhaled loudly. It was midday and I could still see my breath. "Should we continue?" I asked.

"Let's go," Frank said. He popped his last piece of salty meat in his mouth, picked up his pack, and led the hike.

I kept my head down again—it was a strategy that gave me comfort. Or at least kept me sane.

Lillian screamed. My blood turned to ice. I looked up and she was sitting on a rock. She'd collapsed in a crying heap. I ran, but before I could get to her, she started wailing.

"We did it," she cried. "I can't believe it."

"What?"

I picked up my pace. Jagged rocks bore into the soles of my water-soaked boots.

We'd reached the top. The valley below was still green. Autumn hadn't frozen its color away. A large lake sat in the middle of the lush valley.

A hand rested on my shoulder. "Anna," Marshall

whispered into my ear. His breath was hot and made me shiver. "You did it."

"*We* did it," I said. I rested my hand on my belly. "We all did it."

"See that lake?" Marshall pointed. "I bet if we follow that outlet, it will lead us directly to Crempshaw. It probably feeds the log flumes that the camp is so famous for. A short cut."

I turned to Frank. "How long do you think it will take to get to that lake?"

"Roughly two hours." He crossed his arms. "And it looks like it's not that steep or as rocky on the way down."

"I'm thankful for that," Elizabeth said.

"Well," I said. "Let's go."

CHAPTER 44

Frank was wrong. It was just as steep on the way down. The rocks weren't as jagged, but it was still a precarious trek. Falling for probably the twentieth time, a dull pain set into my back. But it wasn't the physical pain that was wearing on me. It was the mental game. Losing my footing every fifty feet, the bone-chilling cold, and the looming fear that Paul was on our heels was wearing on me.

Not to mention, I had no idea what type of toll this was taking on my baby.

"We're almost there," Frank announced. "Once we make it to the lake, we'll start a fire, warm up, and get some food. Sleep will come easy tonight."

The rocks turned to loam as we passed below the tree line. Fresh pine scent calmed my nerves for the moment. After a few hours, we were finally there, but Frank pushed us until we were on the lake's opposite bank. I unwrapped a pack full of dry wood and stacked it. Marshall walked up with his black kettle. Inside were vegetables and other supplies. He pulled them all out and started preparing another stew.

"Did you carry that the whole time?" I asked.

"I did," he said.

"I didn't realize you filled the pot with supplies." I furrowed my brow.

"It freed up a blanket." He cut up a carrot. "And that was paramount."

"I guess," I said, stretching my back. "But you carried that heavy pot, full of supplies, and were Elizabeth's primary crutch?"

He nodded.

"Geez, Marsh," I said. "You're as strong as a lumberjack."

He didn't reply.

"I have something to show you." I took the keringer saber-fang from my pocket. "I got it from the keringer you pushed into the pit. I want you to have it."

"Anna . . ." Marshall turned away. "You earned it. Keep it. Never know when you might need it."

"Sure, Marsh." I left him to cook.

During dinner, I studied the group. We were battered, blistered, and bruised. In addition to their injuries from the keringer, most had cuts on their hands from falling on the way up. A few lay on their stomach to eat because their butts were too sore from falling on the way down. Everyone had their water-soaked shoes off and next to the fire. Red and blistered feet were the number one commonality between us all. Even Elizabeth. Technically speaking, she only had a blistered foot, since she could only walk on one.

The lush green area we'd seen from above was a bit of a mirage. Up close, the grass revealed an even mix of dead and green grass. Fall was here. But I didn't need the foliage to tell that story. The second the sun set, the temperature plummeted. There was no cloud cover to hide the spectacular stars and frigid air.

"Marsh," I said, "do you want to share a blanket tonight?"

He looked at me curiously. "I, uh, no."

"Don't do that." I crossed my arms. "It's cold. If we unpack everything, that just creates more work for us in the morning. Let's just share one. Plus, I could use your body heat again."

Frank chuckled.

"Geez," I interrupted. "Eavesdrop much?"

Frank's face reddened. "If anyone is willing to share blankets tonight, please do. Let's keep the supplies bundled if we can. We'll form a circle around the fire to sleep tonight."

"What about keringer?" Hazel asked. "Will they come around while we sleep?"

"Unlikely," Tommy said. He absently rubbed his arm. "They're typically afraid of fire."

"Typically," she said flatly. Her long brown curls were a frizzy mess.

"I'm going to bed." Tommy waved her off. "There's enough to worry about without bringing up the keringer." His words were sharp. No doubt the pain from the sting in his arm was at the forefront of his mind. And that wasn't even touching the emotional pain I assumed he felt from watching his friend Brad die.

"Good idea," I said. "Let's just get some rest."

I settled by the fire and Marshall lay next to me. His body wasn't radiating heat like it had before. I rolled over to talk to him and was greeted by his feet.

"Whatever," I mumbled. I closed my eyes, buried my head in the blanket, and welcomed the darkness.

Somehow, despite the cold and weirdness from Marshall, I managed to fall into a deep, restful sleep. It felt like I'd been asleep for hours when a hand over my mouth jerked me awake.

CHAPTER 45

My hands pawed at the heavy palm covering my mouth. I struggled and my eyes flew open.

Frank.

He had a finger pressed to his lips. With wide eyes, I nodded.

"Annalise." He pointed to the mountainside; I didn't understand. "Watch."

I stared into the night. My cold breath weaved out between his fingers. The smell of the extinguished fire lingered. He removed his hand from my mouth, and I sat up. A glimpse of orange caught my eye.

There it was.

What I'd been dreading from the moment we left. Torches. In the pit of my stomach, I knew. It had to be my brother. Paul. He'd tracked us. Despite our head start and long days, our series of misfortunes had given him time to catch up with our caravan.

I cursed. "We have to go!"

"I know," Frank said. "I already put out the fire. Hopefully, they didn't already spot us. If we leave now, we might have an hour head start on them."

Marshall stirred. I must have bumped his leg, or he heard us talking. Once awake, he sat up abruptly. The moonlight shone on his dark skin. His eyes widened with shock.

"Marsh," I whispered, "we have to get everyone up." I pointed to the ridge. "It's Paul. They've been following us."

I jumped to my feet.

"No," Frank said harshly. "Don't startle everyone. Let's wake them up individually. The last thing we need is someone screaming. The clear sky will only carry our voices."

He was right. The three of us each went from person to person and carefully woke them up. We packed as quickly as we could. I was thankful we hadn't completely unpacked last night. Score one for me.

Judging by the lavender sky and fading stars, it must have been between four and five in the morning. I wondered if Paul's crew had been walking all night, or just gotten up incredibly early. Either way, it looked like they were on foot now—which wasn't surprising given how steep the mountain was.

"Wait." Marshall stopped abruptly.

"What?" I tugged on his arm. "We have to go."

"No." He pointed at the stream. "They'll catch us in no time. Look how fast they're descending the mountain."

"Yeah," I said. "That's why we need to get out of here."

"Actually . . ." Marshall smiled. "We can do better than that. Tommy?"

"Yes?" he replied.

"Come with me," Marshall said. "Let's walk up this way and throw them off our path. Frank, if you walk in the stream, they will only see our footprints headed in the opposite direction. We'll break a bunch of branches, do whatever we need to do to draw them this way. Then, we'll double back in our same footprints and meet up with you."

"Come on," Hazel whined.

"Wait." Frank opened the map. "They'll see your footprints headed in both directions. That won't work." Frank stroked his beard as he studied the map. "But this might. See this stream?"

"Yes." Marshall stared at the map.

"If you go north and keep that way for a few miles, you'll run into this stream." He pointed. "Leave lots of footprints going into the water. You'll be so far north, they'll think we headed to Camp Louvier via the water. Follow it south until you meet up with the Big Bend River. If you get cold, rest on the rocks. Not the moss. They're great trackers. From there, you'll continue south until you see the stream that feeds Crempshaw Camp's log flumes into the river. You'll have to go upstream, but it'll take you to Crempshaw. Hopefully by tonight."

"That's genius," Lillian said.

"Great idea," Marshall echoed.

"I don't know." I reached down and touched the water. It was cold, maybe forty degrees. "It's really cold, Marsh. I don't think we can walk in it."

"Anna," he said. "What other choice do we have?"

"I guess." I turned to the group. "Are you all okay with this?"

"Yes," Hazel said desperately. "Can we please just leave already?"

"Hurry." I took Marshall's pack from him. "Please don't get caught."

He brushed my cheek with the front of his fingers but said nothing.

Hazel was first to step into the stream. Her body

tremored immediately. The clear water, while beautiful, stung to the core. We had to wade into it until it was up to our shins, so we didn't leave tracks on the side.

I heard a gasp and looked over my shoulder. Frank had scooped up Elizabeth like a bride on her wedding night. Elizabeth more than exceeded the height requirements for a breeder. At six foot three, she was as tall as Marshall, but her 170-pound weight kept her labeled as a scrawn by Paul's standards. *Fool.* She was strong and lean. Valuable. We all were valuable.

Stepping into the stream, I held my breath. Immediately, all heat escaped my body. My feet felt heavy with each step through the water. Drying my boots last night had been a waste of time. I desperately wanted out. With everyone sloshing through the water, we inadvertently kicked it up onto each other. Lapping water wicked its way up my canvas pants. My breath was quick and uneven.

The sun crested over the mountain. We'd gone roughly two miles. The pack on my back dug into my shoulders. Blisters on my feet had long since burst and torn. I was hungry—we'd skipped breakfast.

"I can't feel my feet," someone said.

"Me neither," Lillian said. "I hate to be a bother, but I need to get out of the water soon."

"I agree." I turned to Frank. "Are you good?"

"Yes." He deposited Elizabeth on the bank of the stream and stretched out his back. "Let's break for a moment."

"I don't think I can go on," Hazel said. She collapsed on the riverbed and tucked herself into a ball.

Five women sat down. Several were crying. Others stared blankly into the timber. Hazel's breakdown had caused a chain reaction.

"No." I swore I could feel my brother on my heels. "We're so close. We have to keep going."

"I can't," Hazel sobbed. "I tried. I did my best. I've been attacked by a keringer, twice. I haven't had a proper bath in days." She tugged at her long, frizzy hair. "I'm hungry and tired. I'm not cut out for this."

"Yes, you are," I said. "We're lumberjacks. *All* of us. We're strong, tall and . . . and . . . and if I can do this pregnant, you can do this." I started walking. "Now let's go." Without Marshall, I had to take on the role of coach.

Each step felt like my legs were made of concrete. Then my pants started to freeze. I looked over my shoulder and no one had moved. Not a single one. Crunching leaves and rapid footfalls from up ahead drew my attention away.

Crap.

We were caught.

By . . . Frank? He was running at full speed with a goofy grin plastered to his face.

"Come see," he said.

"When did you run off?" I asked.

"When Hazel was bellyaching," he said. Hazel scowled at him. "I wanted to see what was up ahead."

"Well?"

"Come see," he panted. "For yourself."

I ran up ahead but fell. My feet were numb. I landed on my hands again, protecting my belly. My raw palms stung and the skin broke open. Pulling myself up, I forced my feet forward. The more I moved, the better it seemed to get.

I rounded the corner, and a wooden oasis loomed before me. Long, v-shaped troughs lined the stream. They weaved in and out—some were as high as twenty feet. Water flowed down the troughs. It was only a matter of time before logs careened down it. I stepped back into the freezing river and touched the rough wood flume. It wasn't a mirage. The rough wood was a reality.

Log flumes. We were close.

I turned to run back, but everyone was already behind me. Frank brought up the rear, still helping Elizabeth as her crutch.

"Isn't it amazing?" Frank beamed.

"What is it?" Hazel asked.

"It's a log flume," Frank said. "This is how Crempshaw sends its logs down the river."

Hazel stared blankly at Frank.

"It means we're close," I said. "Can you make it a bit farther, Hazel?"

"I guess."

Walking suddenly didn't feel so exhausting. A few girls hummed and even started singing. My heart fluttered. Finally, a win. All our spirits were lifted for the next half a mile. I just hoped Marshall and Tommy were successful in leading Paul astray.

Lost in thought, I stumbled over a large chunk of wood.

"What the . . ." The ground was wet. Wood was everywhere. Flumes were destroyed. Logs jammed in the flumes had fallen along the riverbed and littered the ground like trash.

"I, um—Frank?"

"Something is wrong," he said.

CHAPTER 46

The panic was palpable. Water trickled loudly where we should have heard tools buzzing and crews singing.

"Who destroyed this?" Lillian asked.

"It doesn't look intentional," Frank said.

"Oh my," Elizabeth gasped. "Was it a keringer?"

"No," I said. "Of course not. Why would a keringer destroy the log flumes?"

"I—I can't do it again." Elizabeth collapsed. Her shoulders heaved as she cried hysterically and held her injured leg. "They're everywhere. The timber isn't safe. Nowhere is safe."

I clenched my jaw and ran over to her. "Elizabeth," I said. "Pull yourself together." I tried yanking her to her feet, but she was too heavy. I resorted to rubbing her back with the palm of my good hand. Dirt smeared across the rough material of her shirt. "It's okay. Think about it. A keringer wouldn't destroy a log flume for fun. And look, parts of the flume are completely ruined, and other parts are untouched."

She stopped crying long enough to look. "Then what?" she sniffled.

"It was probably a twister," I said. I hoped. "You know how random they can be."

"Maybe," she said. "But the trees around it aren't destroyed."

Fear was written all over her face. How could I blame her? She'd fallen into a pit and seen the bones. Smelled the death. And the cave. It only proved what we feared. The keringer were not only strong, but also smart. That cave led somewhere. A secret tunnel, perhaps? They were capable of critical thinking. Organized.

"Please." I tilted her chin up, fearful if she looked down, she'd start sobbing again. "We have to go. Marshall and Tommy are risking everything to ensure our safe passage."

"She's right," Lillian said, her voice unsteady. "We have to go. Right now, we're sitting ducks. You can do it, I believe in you."

"Elizabeth." I stood. "Once we get there, the people of Crempshaw will tell us all about what happened here. Let's let them fill in the blanks."

Frank had walked over and helped me lift her. She reluctantly placed her good leg on the ground and started limping. I knew we were close and prayed we'd get there before anyone else freaked out.

Within five minutes, Hazel crushed my twister theory.

"Why isn't anyone out here fixing it?" she asked.

"Maybe camp was damaged too, and they're fixing that first." I stared forward. Why was she asking me? It wasn't like I had the answers.

"If their camp is destroyed, then we'll have nowhere to go!" Hazel said.

Elizabeth was in full hysterics now. She was still trying to walk while crying and sniffling.

"Hazel." I rushed back to her. "Knock it off," I whispered to her. "You're scaring everyone. Elizabeth is traumatized, and you're making it worse."

"I just—"

"No," I interrupted. "We're so close. What other option do we have? To turn back?"

Frank scooped Elizabeth up once more. "Exhaustion is taking over. Let me carry you the last leg," he said. "Sorry for the pun." He laughed.

"Watch your hands." Elizabeth's face flushed and the tears stopped.

"Right." He smiled at her.

While Frank was tending to Elizabeth, I ran to the front. To lead. It made sense. This whole harebrained idea was mine in the first place. I should be the one to walk us into Crempshaw. Explain ourselves.

I nodded at the women as I passed them but made sure to avoid any conversation. The closer we got, the more destruction we saw. It was apparent the flumes had been destroyed by something very large. With clawed hands. And possibly saber-fangs.

I sucked in a deep breath of the cool autumn air, held it in, and closed my eyes. Once again, I was faced with a situation where I had no choice. Injured, bloody, and nearly out of rations, we had to press forward. But if there was a band of keringer to face, well . . . I guess it was better than Paul releasing us.

Just beyond a thick outcropping of trees stood our sanctuary.

Crempshaw.

The camp was bigger than Younish. And it was square, not like the round camp I'd lived my entire life in. It was still a couple hundred yards away, but the destruction was clear even from a distance. The gates to the front hung askew. Large holes roughly six feet up punctured the wooden spires. Had the keringer jumped *through* the walls? I had never heard of a keringer attacking a camp before. And this wasn't *one* keringer, but appeared to be the work of several.

"Everyone," I whispered loudly, "follow me." I rushed back into the water, behind a broken log flume. I hoped they hadn't seen the veracity of the destruction before I could warn them.

Sloshing feet and grumbles met me, hidden from clear view.

"What is it?" Lillian asked.

"I need to go up ahead."

"What?" Frank asked.

"The camp." I paused. Floating, broken bits of wood lapped against my boots. "It's been attacked. I need to see how badly, if there are survivors, or if it has been completely abandoned."

"Attacked by what?" Elizabeth said slowly.

"You were right." I kicked the water. "It looks like the camp was attacked by a band of freaking keringer."

"I knew it!" she screamed.

"Shh," I said harshly. "We don't know if there are still keringer present. Heck, this attack could have been recent. I'm not risking your lives for mine. Just stay here and watch for Tommy and Marshall. Don't let them go into the camp until I get back."

"I'm coming with you," Frank said.

"Are you sure?" I asked. His presence would put my mind a little at ease, but I didn't want to put him in harm's way.

"Yes." He rummaged through our scattered supplies on the edge of the water. "Here." He handed me an ax. "We need to be prepared. But carry it over your shoulder like a jack, in case there are people still there. I don't want them to think we're hostile."

"Good idea," I said. "We'll be back." I turned and

exited the water. My heart pounded in my chest. My mouth was devoid of saliva.

* * *

"Annalise," Frank said. "This is bad."

"Thank you, Captain Obvious."

"I'm serious." He pointed to the askew gates. "Whatever happened here, it was recent. Do you smell that?"

"What? Am I hard of smelling?" I gagged. "Of course I smell it."

Death. Rotting flesh. It didn't need an explanation. We were only a few feet from the entrance. It was now or never. I stole a look at Frank. He was stoic, expressionless.

Walking through the gates was uneventful. The silence was deafening. Crempshaw was, indeed, a superior camp. Several large, wooden buildings were set up throughout the camp. Although many were damaged, you could see what once stood. Polished wood, shingled roofs. Younish had no permanent structures. Just tents.

Then I saw it. A dozen or so bodies rotting on the ground. Flesh ripped from bodies. Entire rib cages exposed. Others faces had been distorted beyond recognition. Many were missing limbs. My stomach churned at the gruesome sight.

I turned to Frank but said nothing.

Halfway through camp, on the right side, were trampled fruit trees. The black soil, rich with nutrients, was a luxury I'd never experienced. There were even rudimentary oil lights mounted on the doorways to each building. Real ones, not just a bonfire and torches. Shards of broken glass were scattered under some of the destroyed modern lights.

A tall tower with a wooden wheel caught my eye. A large, square opening at the top revealed the beginning of the log flume, the breadcrumbs that lead us to Crempshaw. Two enormous circular saws were atop the tower. A sawmill. The log elevator's ropes had been cut, with the ends frayed. One lone pine tree grew tall in the middle of the camp.

Deeper in camp, I saw another sawmill attached to log flumes. One was on the front left side, the flumes leading out into the water. The other was kitty-corner, in the back-right corner of camp. I assumed the flumes exited the back side.

The remnants of the battle were apparent. Blood spattered across the fronts of buildings. Shoes, clothes, broken bottles, and other debris littered the ground. A few buildings still smoldered on the other end of camp. The combination of death and smoke churned my stomach. I slipped a mint from my tin and greedily chomped on it, holding the bile in the back of my throat.

Rustling near a collapsed structure grabbed my attention. I looked at Frank. His ax was held above him. Ready to attack. Gripping my ax, I did the same.

I did my best to steady my breathing, but it was a lost cause.

"Hello?" I said, my voice shaky. "Is anyone there?"

A hand reached out from the rubble. I rushed over and pushed a few boards off the person. A woman crawled out using her forearms, then stood and dusted off her dirty overalls. Her long, gray braids were frizzy and disheveled. She was bloody, but most of it appeared to be dried.

"Are you okay?" I asked. "What happened?"

She tried to speak and collapsed into my arms.

CHAPTER 47

My knees buckled. I slowly guided the woman to the ground.

"Get her some water," I yelled to Frank.

He rushed over to a well. The stone side was partially caved, but the opening was undamaged. Frank dropped the bucket and wheeled it up.

"Here." He sloshed the full pail at me.

I tipped her chin up, and she blinked wildly at me. I handed her a ladle, but she pushed it aside and took the whole bucket. A wound on her lip reopened, and blood dripped down her chin into the water. She paused only to take a deep breath.

"Thank you." She gently touched her lip as she stared forward. "Who are you?"

"My name is Annalise. And this is Frank. Your color is coming back. I'm sorry, I didn't catch your name."

"Patricia." She shook her head and squeezed her eyes shut. "Where did you come from?"

"We came from Younish Camp," Frank said, standing. "It's a little over one hundred miles away."

"Younish?" Her eyes grew wide. "Home of the disgusting breeder program. What do you want with Crempshaw?"

"That's actually why we're here," I started. "We're

seeking asylum from Lumberchief Paul. We don't believe in it either. There are nineteen of us in total."

"Nineteen?" She scanned the area. "Where?"

"They're outside camp," Frank said. "We saw the destruction and, well, we weren't sure what we were walking into."

"Patricia." I placed my hands on top of hers. "What happened here?"

"The keringer," she gasped. "They . . . they got loose."

"Loose?" Frank pinched his brow.

"Yes." She slowly stood. "It was a few nights ago. The lightning storm. It spooked them."

"I'm sorry," I said. "You'll need to back up. It sounds like they were loose *inside* your camp?"

"We captured three of them," she said. "We wanted to tame them. Use them like cattle. It was foolish, I suppose. They were secure in their cages, I swear. But they lost their minds during that storm. I'd never seen anything like it.

"It all happened so fast," she continued. "Once they broke through their cages, they were mad. Jumping about, thrashing and destroying any and everything they could. Gas lights were knocked over, fires spread. It was chaos. People were gored and stomped to death. They killed so many of us. I think a few ran away, but I can't be sure. I was trapped under the debris. Didn't have a great vantage point." Her eyes filled with tears.

"Where are they?" I asked carefully. "The rest of the bodies."

"I wasn't finished." She shook her head. "Once the keringer escaped, I thought it was over. But every night, they came back. The beasts. Scavenging. They'd drag body after body away. I was trapped under the wood, and they never sniffed me out. They were looking for the dead, I suppose."

"They came back?" Frank asked. "More than once? Where are the drag marks?"

"Geez, Frank," I said out the side of my mouth. "Have a little tact."

"Yes." Patricia inhaled deeply, regaining her composure. "They've been back the last three evenings. It rained last night. It was the only thing that saved me. I was able to drink a bit of the rain water. It cleansed the ground. You said there were others?" she asked.

"Yes," I said. "I think you should sit. When was the last time you ate?"

"Three days ago. Before this happened." She waved me off. "Go get them, your crew. We have to repair the gate and patch the holes. A fire, yes! A fire. We need to build one before night falls or they'll be back." She was frantic.

"Of course." I turned to Frank. "Can you get the women and fill them in?"

He nodded and jogged away.

I pulled a hunk of pemmican from my pocket and handed it to her. "Take a minute and I'll go gather some supplies." I stopped short. "And where would that be?"

"I'll show you." She walked me over to a partially intact building near a sawmill. She was almost as tall as me, and nearly as robust. Her two long, gray braids cascaded to the middle of her back. "I already miss those damn things." She pointed.

"The sawmills?" I asked. "You worked in there?"

"What?" she asked. "Because I'm old you don't think I can run one?"

"No, not at all." I stopped and faced her. "In Younish, even before the Scrawn Law, women weren't allowed to run heavy equipment."

"Girl, boy, young, or old." Deep crow's feet emerged with her smile. "We're all the same here. And for the record, I'm sixty."

"Wow." I started walking. "You're so, um, spry."

"My secret? Never stop moving, I suppose. Everyone here is like me. Or at least, they were."

"Annalise," Frank yelled.

I glanced over my shoulder. Frank was in the distance with the rest of the women. "Over here." I waved with both arms.

I walked into a partially collapsed storage building. Full of saws, lumber, nails, and hammers, we'd be able to quickly repair the holes.

"Patricia." I picked up a fallen board. "There are sixteen women and three men. Some of the women are pregnant. I hope that's okay."

"As long as they can swing a hammer, they're fine by me."

"Ladies"—Frank poked his head in—"this is who I told you about. Patricia, the only survivor."

"How did you do it?" Hazel asked. "I've actually been attacked by a keringer twice."

I rolled my eyes.

"I can't believe the keringer came back," another exclaimed.

"What about—"

"I can answer all your questions." Patricia held up her hands. "But we must get the camp secure before nightfall."

"She's right," Frank said. "Let's get the gates up, holes covered, and a fire built. I'm sure Patricia wouldn't mind recounting what happened over dinner."

I picked up a few two-by-fours and walked to a large gash in the wall. Frank walked toward the gate. Leaving the heavy lifting to him was fine by me.

"Anna," a man yelled.

I didn't need to turn to see who it was. I knew. *Marshall.*

I dropped my hammer and ran to him.

"You made it," I said. It felt like I'd been holding my breath all day and I could finally exhale. "Tommy . . ." I nodded at him.

"Just barely." Tommy rubbed his eyes. "I hope we led Paul away."

"How much time do you think it bought us?"

"A day," Marshall said. "Maybe less. What—what happened here?"

"Keringer," I said.

"Keringer?" Tommy echoed.

"Tommy, Marshall." Frank clapped both men on the back. "I knew you'd make it. Come help me with the gate, I'll explain."

Marshall walked away but looked at me over his shoulder. Those big, sad brown eyes. I thought arriving at Crempshaw would snap him back to the old Marsh. But it didn't. I knew it, and he knew it: The real danger still loomed.

The whir of saws and hammers was nearly deafening. Renewed hope seemed to energize us all. Holes were quickly patched. Areas cleaned up. Overturned water collectors were righted.

Elizabeth used a plank of wood as a makeshift crutch. "Annalise, I think I found the food supply. A few girls are organizing it and separating out the rancid and damaged supplies."

"That's excellent news." I helped her sit on a stump.

"Thank you."

"Rest for a while." I gingerly elevated her leg onto a log. "I'm going to go start a fire."

Dragging wood into the center of the camp reminded me of the poor souls whose bodies had been dragged away by the keringer. My heart sank. So many people had died at the hands of Paul, and it was intentional. The keringer attacks felt just as senseless. The residents of Crempshaw were simply trying to find a use for them, and it had cost them dearly. I sucked in a deep breath and immediately regretted it. We'd need to do something with the remaining bodies, and soon. Based on the sun's position, we only had a few hours of daylight.

Marshall wrapped a torn cloth around a piece of wood and dipped it in gasoline. The lumber was stacked eight feet high in the shape of a teepee. Stacks of reserve wood were piled safely away. All that was left was for Marshall to set the fire.

A whoosh of fire swept up the tall tower and became our protector from keringer. At least we hoped. The gentle crackle and scent of freshly burnt wood made it feel like home. I stroked my belly as I stared at the dancing flames.

"We need to bury the dead," I said. "Then we'll meet back at the fire."

It was the second time in two days that I was creating a makeshift cemetery. I hoped it would be my last. But I knew better.

This was a task done in silence. Holes were dug outside of the walls; remains of crushed, gored, slashed, and disfigured bodies were gently placed into shallow graves. The ones that had been exposed to the sunlight were worse off. We had to be especially careful with those bodies, for fear the limbs would break off when we lifted them.

Once finished, we all met up at the troughs by the out-houses. We did our best to wash the death off our faces, arms, and hands. I walked to the bonfire and found most of the group already seated.

Patricia stood and explained to the rest what had happened and how the keringer had come back night after night. She answered questions and remained stoic. Marshall sat next to me.

"How are you feeling?" he asked.

"Tired."

Marshall turned my legs so they were facing him, then unlaced my boots.

"You should elevate your feet." He rested my sweaty feet on the tops of his thighs.

"Gross." I tried to pull them away. "I'm sure they smell." I faintly heard a woman asking Patricia another question, but my mind was elsewhere. "What's next?"

"I don't know," Marshall said. "We have to figure this out."

"I know," I said. I slammed my feet onto the ground. "Look at us, Marsh, we can't fight."

"We can try." He picked my legs back up. "But it would be a last resort."

"Let me think." I closed my eyes. Marshall rubbed my feet. I didn't deserve him. Not even as a friend. "What if we set traps?"

"What kind of traps?" He tilted his ear toward his shoulder.

"Traps." I waved my arms. "Like the kind you hunt with. We can set ones that kill or capture. But human-sized."

"That is a great idea." He raised his voice. "Every-one, Paul will most likely be here in the next twenty-four hours. We need to prepare."

"How?" Hazel crossed her arms.

"I'm glad you asked, Hazel," Marshall said. "We've got a plan. We're going to trap Paul and his mechanicals."

"Okay, how?" Tommy asked.

"We're going to outsmart Paul," Marshall said.

"That shouldn't be hard," I mumbled.

CHAPTER 48

"What did you have in mind?" Frank asked.

"Well . . ." I scrambled for an idea. "We could dig a big hole."

"A hole?" Hazel rolled her eyes. "That's all you got. Wow, great idea."

"It *is* a great idea, Hazel. Thank you," I said. "We'll make it deep, and big. At the bottom, there'll be spikes. But we'll cover the top with pine boughs. When they step in, bam! They get impaled."

"Kind of like the keringer pit." Elizabeth shuddered.

"Yeah." I gave her a lopsided grin. "Sorry."

"Yes," Frank said. "I like that. What if we take the bolts out of the saws on the sawmills? We can turn them on, and the saws will come flying out. Those saws are jagged, sharp, and deadly."

"This will make it awfully dangerous for us to navigate throughout camp, I suppose," Patricia said.

"True, but we'll have someone man the station." Frank rubbed his beard. "And we could string ropes above camp and hook a pulley to it. We'll get around camp that way. No one will need to cross on foot."

"That's perfect," I said. "Anyone else?" I looked around at a bunch of blank stares. The momentum was over almost as fast as it began. Coming up with another idea was critical. "Okay, uh, how about, yeah . . . So, how about we reroute a flume, pile up a bunch of logs, then set one in the front to hold them back. When they get close, we'll let them loose. Just think, a bunch of huge logs careening down directly at them."

"Where will we get the logs?" Hazel asked.

"Check the area, or cut down a damn tree," I said. "In case you haven't noticed, we're surrounded by them."

"How about a catapult?" Lillian asked. "We could build a few and heave boulders at them."

"Sure," I said. "If we have time to build some, that will be great. Anyone else?"

Silence.

"Okay, then." I stood. It felt like stepping on a thousand needles. "Let's get to work. Marsh, can you loosen the bolts on the sawmills?

"Of course." He turned to Patricia. "Can you show me the way? I'm not familiar with your type of mill."

"Yes." She nodded. "You might need my assistance. The saws are six feet in diameter."

"Who wants to dig another hole?" I asked.

"I'll lead the charge," Frank said.

"Me too," a few others chimed in.

"Excellent." I looked to my left. "That's the supply shed. Let's dig the hole in front of the fire near the entrance, get as many as we can when they walk in. I guess we can cover it with skinny branches, then leaves and dirt to conceal it. Tommy?"

"Yes?"

"Can you work on the ropes above and create a pulley system?"

"Sure thing," he said. "I just hope there's enough rope in the shed."

"Me too." I walked over with him to see what we

were working with. "If not, we'll really have to be careful or we'll sabotage ourselves."

On my way to the shed, I encountered Elizabeth crouched in the corner.

"Elizabeth, what are you doing?"

"Hiding." She rested her elbows on her knees and stared at the ground. "I can't help with anything. I feel so useless."

"That's not true," I said. "Actually, I have the perfect job for you." She perked up a little. "Now that we have the fire going, we can bring some food over to you, and you can make us a stew. Heck, that's probably the most important job of the day."

"I'm not a great cook," she said. "But I can try. At least I can do that sitting."

"Exactly." I helped her to her feet. "Find a comfy spot by the fire, and we'll bring the stuff to you."

She hobbled away. I hoped she wouldn't ruin dinner. My stomach grumbled just at the thought of food. We'd likely have to work all night long just to get this done, but the fire and noise would probably keep the keringer away.

"Jackpot," Tommy said. He lifted a tarp and there were hundreds of feet of rope below it.

"Excellent," I said. "Did you have someone in mind that you'd like to help you?"

"Not really," he said. "But I can ask someone. Especially if that means it frees you up to get Elizabeth something to cook for us." His face blossomed with red. "Sorry, I wasn't, I . . . I'm just starving."

"You and me both, buddy."

"Hazel," I yelled.

She yelled over her shoulder, "Yeah?"

"Can you get together with Elizabeth and bring her whatever she needs to make us dinner?"

With arms crossed, she shrugged her pointy shoulders and walked away. That girl was testing every ounce of patience I had left.

My eyes grew wide, and the smile on my face broadened as I scanned the area. I was so impressed.

Until I wasn't.

A group of women had gone to the front corner and stacked logs on the flume. Watching them, it became apparent to me it was going to take much longer than I hoped. Once they'd get more than five stacked, they'd come crashing down. Frustration was mounting, but furthermore, it was dangerous. I half waited for one of them to get crushed. It sounded like an easy task, but it kept falling apart. Literally. That combined with the exhaustion and stress of Paul and the keringer was enough to keep us all on edge.

Frank and his group weren't faring much better. The hole was riddled with roots and rocks. They'd barely made any headway.

"How's it go—" I started.

Frank let out a string of curse words that left me embarrassed and slightly impressed. I turned on my heel and walked toward the sawmills. Although it'd been a few days since they were in use, the air still lingered of freshly cut wood now that the bodies were gone.

"Hello?" I poked my head in.

"I'll leave you two to talk, I suppose," Patricia said.

"Marsh?" I pinched my brow. "What was that all about?"

"It's these blades." He walked out from behind the massive machine, wiping his greasy hands on a towel. "They go the opposite direction."

I tilted my head in confusion.

"If we turn them on as it stands, they'll come careening directly at us," he said.

"Oh."

"Yeah." He walked back to the machine and started hitting something. A metallic clink echoed. "I need to figure out how to reverse the engine."

"Wait," I said. "Didn't you say one of the women was a mechanic? Or her dad was or something?"

"Unfortunately . . ." He paused. "That is Elizabeth, and she's not much use right now."

"Crap. And we can't take Frank off of digging that hole."

I stared at him, hoping he'd say it was all going to be okay.

He didn't.

"This is going to take at least half a day to figure out, then repeat on the other sawmill."

"We don't have that kind of time, Marsh."

"I know." He raised his voice. "But what other choice do we have?" He turned toward me and rested his thick hands on my shoulders. "We might have to abandon this part of the plan."

"No." I bit my lip. "Keep working. I'll bring you some dinner. I know you'll get this done in time. I believe in you."

"I'm glad someone does," he said.

"What?"

"Nothing," he mumbled, and turned back to the saw.

"Marsh, I don't have the right words to make this better. I'm sorry." I wrapped my arms around him from behind and squeezed. "This all sucks. And we can't catch a break. We can't just hide. They'll find us when they arrive."

He loosened my grip and turned so he was facing me. "That was the most violent hug I've ever received."

"I want things to get better," I said.

"I know you do." He placed a gentle kiss on my forehead and turned back to the saw.

I walked out.

"Annalise—" Tommy was completely out of breath. "I've been looking for you."

"Oh no." I squeezed my eyes shut. "What now?"

"When I was on top, making the pulley system, I saw—"

"A keringer?" I sucked in a breath.

"Worse." He rested his hands on his knees, regaining his composure. "Torches. They found us."

CHAPTER 49

"Gates! Get those gates closed, now!" I yelled.

I ran as quickly as my bad leg would allow. My chest burned, and I noticed for the first time that my belly needed support. This was new. I didn't like it.

"Everyone hide!" I turned to Patricia. "Is there another way out?"

"Yes," she said. "But it's all the way in the back. I'm not sure if it's been damaged. Using it should be a last resort, I suppose."

"Hide!" I yelled again.

Marshall ran behind the door of the sawmill. The women working on the logs hid behind their large pile. Tommy shimmied up the lone tree in camp. Frank sprinted toward Elizabeth, scooped her up, and deposited both himself and Elizabeth into the hole. A few girls followed suit. I ran behind the supply shed.

"Hello?" I heard a deep voice bellow.

My chest tightened and my ears tingled. It was happening, and we weren't ready. My hands shook.

Rocks came flying over the walls and landed with a thud. A chainsaw whirred to life.

"Identify yourself," the voice yelled again.

Paul sounded different. Sober.

Muffled voices murmured near the gate. How many were in the army? Tears welled in my eyes.

Patricia popped up and ran toward the gate.

"Patricia," I whispered loudly. "What are you doing?"

She tugged on the gate, opening it for the intruders. Happy cries and hugs started almost at once. I couldn't hear what they said, but it sounded light. Cheerful. It hit me. This was a reunion. The people who ran during the attack. They were back. And now we were the intruders to them. All nineteen of us.

Patricia had been welcoming. After all, we freed her from being trapped. But the others might not be as happy to have us. More mouths to feed. Bodies to clothe. Babies to birth.

As they moved closer to the fire ring, I stared at their faces. Their clothes were ripped, torn, and bloodied, faces haggard, bodies injured. Their weapons had dried blood and hair on them. Their expressions were hopeful but had an underlying melancholy. Some were limping, others cradling maimed appendages. But nonetheless, the return seemed happy and optimistic. I counted them; there were twelve in total. Eight men and four women. The women holding the whirring chainsaw turned it off.

A rustle behind me grabbed my attention. Hazel emerged from her hiding spot. I raised a finger to my lips and motioned for her to lie back down. Damn Hazel. Patricia gestured wildly in my direction, but never looked at me. I stayed hidden.

She held her hands up in a defensive position and walked swiftly along the group, carefully guiding them around the hole Frank had dug. Her face wore a mask of worry. Crap. I stepped out from behind the shed and dropped an ax I'd been holding.

"Hello." My arms hung limply, and empty palms faced forward. "My name is Annalise. I come from Younish Camp."

My words were answered with raised axes, blood-stained chains, and knives. Fire danced across their faces. Their expressions were hard.

"No." Patricia stepped in front of them. "Drop your weapons. This is what I was trying to tell you." She firmly placed her hands on a man's ax and forced it to the ground. "I said drop it."

Out of the corner of my eye, Frank popped up from his spot. I raised my left hand slightly and subtly shook my head. *Not yet.*

I needed to smooth everything over before I revealed the entire crew. If they attacked me, we'd still have the element of surprise on our side. They could run away or save me. Either way, it gave them options.

Unless Frank blew it for us.

CHAPTER 50

We were at a stalemate. They didn't know what to do with me. No one said anything; they simply stared.

Marshall stepped out from behind the sawmill door, his chest puffed out, hands at his sides. Frank had laid back down, but his head was still visible to me.

Patricia stepped toward me and rested a hand on my shoulder. "This is Annalise. This is who I was telling you about, Doc," she said, turning to me. "Annalise, you were right to build the fire. They saw it and guessed it was safe to return."

"That's Annalise?" He pointed at me. He looked to be in his sixties like Patricia. But also like Patricia, he was in great shape. Strong and full. Tan skin told me he was still active in lumberjacking. His short, frizzy white hair and deep wrinkles showed his age. "I thought you were a man for a moment," he mumbled.

I answered with a smile. Marsh had done a good job of turning me into a boy.

Frank popped up, ax in hand. "She's a woman, and she's with—"

Doc and his friends raised their weapons.

"Frank," I yelled. "Lose the ax."

He complied. Reluctantly.

"How much do they know?" I asked Patricia.

"We already know about the breeding program," Doc said. "There have been rumors about it for weeks. I can't believe it's true."

Frank walked toward Doc with his hand out. "Then you know enough to know we seek refuge—not to overtake or control, but to coexist." He took Doc's hand in his own and shook it. "The name is Frank Janssen. Born and raised in Younish. Broke my heart to see what it's become. I, along with Annalise and Marshall, devised a plan to escape Younish."

"And come here?" Doc raised an eyebrow. "Why here?"

"Proximity, mostly," I said. "And we had always heard how it was clean, disease free, fair, and free of mechanicals."

I shuddered.

"Mechanicals." A thin man stepped forward. His skin was dark, not by sun but by heritage. It wasn't as dark as Marshall's, though. Heavy canvas clothes hung off his bony body. "We've heard of them before. That can't be real, can it? Cutting off parts of your body like that?"

"Sadly, yes." I looked down. "It was initially done to help lumberjacks injured in the timber. But Paul—" I shook my head. "The lumberchief, he started doing it to perfectly healthy people. That was about the time he started the breeding program."

The thin man looked at me with both sadness and skepticism. I walked toward him.

"I'm Annalise." I held out a hand. He stared at it.

"José."

He never shook my hand.

"Let me introduce everyone. Maybe that will put your minds at ease. If we wanted to harm you or steal your camp, we would have attacked you. But we didn't.

We want to help and join your camp. And we just doubled your population. You'll see."

I called out to Tommy. He shimmied down from his hiding spot. I called for the rest of the camp, and they all came forward. Doc's eyes widened. We exchanged names and I led them toward the fire as they talked.

The other two men were large and muscular. They had similar builds to Frank and Tommy. Paul would have classified them, along with three of the four women, as breeders. I hated that I knew that fact. The fourth woman appeared to be a cook. She was slight and wore an apron. Her hair was pinned tightly back. Little did she know, she was about to exchange that apron for a shield. A warrior. A fighter.

After the introductions, an awkward silence fell over the group. Food. That was always a good icebreaker.

"How about some stew?" I suggested.

"Yes," José said. "That would be appreciated. It smells . . . uh, like food."

He was right. It didn't smell delicious, but edible. That was enough. Marshall took over, sampling the soup and adding a few spices until he was satisfied. Elizabeth seemed thankful to be off kitchen patrol and sat near the fire. Marshall spooned up the soup in the dishes we'd brought, along with carved wooden bowls from Crempshaw's kitchen. Well, the ones that weren't broken.

The silence was replaced by chewing and people complimenting Marshall and thanking Elizabeth for the stew. I had to admit, I was thankful Marshall fixed it and made it delicious. I was about to ask them to risk everything for complete strangers. Food was a good gesture.

"As you can see"—I moved my food to my cheek as I spoke, never looking up—"we are preparing for both the keringer and Lumberchief Paul."

It still felt weird calling Paul a lumberchief. Walter was the lumberchief, not Paul. A small pit formed in my stomach.

"The keringer will stay away now," Doc said. "They are afraid of fire."

"But they've been back night after night," Patricia said. "They've been dragging out the dead. They might come back, I suppose."

"Doubtful," a man called Kirkham said. He was big, nearly seven feet tall and thick as a tree. His short blond hair was slicked back.

"Well," I said. "Either way, we need to keep both the keringer and Paul at bay. We think he's been tracking us. Once we got over the mountain, Marshall and Tommy left footprints for them to follow in the wrong direction. We walked in the stream to conceal ours. They did the same thing once they reached a stream that led back this way."

"Clever," Doc said.

"Hopefully, that bought us a day," Frank said.

"Then you may stay the night." Doc placed his bowl down and locked eyes with me. "At first light, you must leave."

I looked to Frank, then Patricia, then back to Frank.

"Leave?" I asked.

"We have been through enough." Kirkham slammed down a fist onto his stump. It shook and nearly broke.

Doc slowly waved his hand up and down at Kirkham, silencing him. "The keringer attacks were upsetting, to say the least. We are peaceful people here at Crempshaw. This sort of thing may be normal for you, but it is not for us. We will not—*cannot*—sustain more violence."

"You don't have a choice!" I stood. "Look around you. You may cast us out, but Paul will still come. He'll break into your camp and steal what he wants, kill whomever gets in his way.

"And you." I pointed to Kirkham. "And Harriet, and you, and the rest of you!" I waved my finger at the three bigger women. I had forgotten all but Harriet's name. "You will all be taken or killed. Look at you. You're large—heck, Harriett, you and your friends are as big as lumberjacks. You know what Paul calls you?"

They all stared at me, eyes wide. Fearful.

"Breeders!"

"Breeders," Harriet said carefully. She and the other two women wore short brown hair that poked only an inch or two out of their beanies. They wore the same clothes as the lumberjacks. Canvas pants, long johns, and heavy shirts.

"Breeders," I repeated. "You'll be forced to have children with a man he deems fit, not a man of your choosing. And if you birth prematurely, he will release you and your baby. *Kill* you and your baby." The words tasted harsh on my tongue. "But before he does that, he'll throw a potlatch. Let everyone get nice and drunk. Then he'll tie you to a platform, and you'll give birth in front of everyone. Force your hand into an iron fist holding an ax. Once your arm becomes too weak, chop!" I swung my arm down. A few people jumped in surprise. "You will decapitate your own baby. Then he'll do the same to you.

"How do I know?" Tears welled up in my eyes. "Because we've witnessed him do it to women who weren't allowed to be pregnant. Scrawn is what he calls us. José and, sorry, I forgot your name." I pointed to the woman wearing the apron. "That would be your fate."

"My name is Frances," she said meekly. "Is this true? It . . . it can't be."

"It's true," Frank said. "All of it."

"You've put us in a very precarious position," Doc said.

"I'm sorry for that," I said. "But we've also helped you."

"Yes." Patricia placed a hand on Doc's knee. "They saved my life. And repaired the walls of camp. The fire will keep us safe, and the food has warmed our bellies. Given us strength."

"She has forced our hand," Kirkham said.

"Now, now." Doc's voice was old and deep. "What's done is done."

"It was only a matter of time, I suppose," Patricia said. "If he's as power hungry as you say he is, he'd come for us or our camp eventually. It's quite superior to most, and we have the log flumes. No one works the timber as efficiently as us."

Doc closed his eyes and nodded.

Of course. The whole purpose of the breeding program wasn't just to get rid of me. It was bigger than that. I was just a speedbump. He wanted more. Why hadn't I seen that?

"We have to prepare."

CHAPTER 51

As daylight broke, my heart sunk. Stupidly, I had thought the work would have gone quicker, and we would have had time to rest. Just as well, I supposed. It wasn't like any of us would have really slept knowing Paul and his brigade could've shown up at any minute.

I walked through camp checking each trap and reviewing the plan with everyone. Turned out, the stragglers of Crempshaw Camp were our lifeline. Amazingly, everything was set. Ready. We were saving each other.

"Hey, Marsh." I sat on a log next to the fire. "Making breakfast?"

"Yep," he said. "I wish they still had chickens. Eggs would have been a nice treat."

"Oatmeal?" I wrinkled my nose.

"Yes." He stirred the pot. The handle on his spoon looked heavy and was caked with thick oats. "But they have sugar, so we're still in for a treat."

"That's great, Marsh," I said. I raised my hand to put it on his shoulder but stopped. Instead, I faked an awkward stretch and abandoned the idea.

The smell of freshly cooked oats and brewed coffee wafted through camp. People slowly gathered near the fire. They were hunched over, blankets wrapped around their shoulder and eyes rimmed with red.

"How are you feeling?" he whispered. "How is the baby?"

"He's getting big." I cradled my stomach. "I'm getting big. So, good, I guess?"

"You're certain it's a boy?"

"Yep." The right side of my lip pulled into an unnatural grin. "Plus, I felt weird calling it an 'it'."

Marshall stared at me, and I couldn't read his expression. He was confusing when it came to the baby. The only thing that was clear was he was protective of him.

"If things go sideways, you run," he said. "Get out of here."

"Marsh," I sucked in a sharp breath. "If it comes down to that, I'll surrender. Give myself up in return for the rest of everyone's safety."

"Not going to happen," Frank interrupted. He stared forward and sipped his coffee. "We're not going to lose anyway. Paul's crew is going to come in tired, and hopefully drunk. We're ready for this. No one dies. No way. No how."

"See?" I shrugged. "It's a non-issue." I stood and hugged Marshall. My swollen belly bumped his stomach, and he took a small step back. It was funny, I'd always heard women say they suddenly 'popped,' and started to show. It was true. He looked down at it, then wrapped his arms around me. "Thank you. For everything."

He pulled away and gave me a sad smile. I'd seen that expression so many times in the last week. A face I didn't recognize. Even when our lives were turned upside down, he never cracked. But with me? The baby? He couldn't fake it. A hitch caught in my throat. I turned.

"Everything good, Doc?" I had to get away from Marshall. The guilt was overwhelming.

"It is," he said. "As good as it can get."

"Okay, then." I turned to the entire group. "I'm going to take my breakfast up on the top of the log flume."

"I don't believe in your condition"—Patricia nodded at my midsection—"that's a wise idea."

I felt singled out. But I was the only visibly pregnant woman doing dangerous things.

"Thank you, Patricia." I clenched my jaw through a forced smile. "But I'll be fine. I need the fresh air. And I think that's the direction they'll be coming."

"*If* they're coming," Kirkham said.

"Oh, they're coming," I said. Now was probably not the best time to tell them we had left behind a straggler. Stephen. We still didn't know if he'd gotten cold feet or been drunk and forgot. Either way, he knew our plan. The question was if he had spilled the beans. Our only saving grace was Marshall and Tommy leading them in a different path. As if we'd changed our minds. "Paul will be here. And you need to get in that headspace."

I picked up a bowl of thick oatmeal. The ceramic warmed my hands. I didn't bother turning as I yelled over my shoulder, "Better be ready for a battle."

CHAPTER 52

The view from the top of the log flume, which was hooked to the tower in the sawmill, was vast. I threw down a few signals to Marshall. He relayed them to the group. After ten minutes or so, we had our system figured out. Two groups of survivors had become one. And we had our own language. Sort of.

Now, up high and at the front of camp, I could see the destruction from another angle. Smashed buildings. Broken fences. Traces of blood. Our repairs were obvious, and the few bodies that had remained left death marks— even after the rain. How had a few keringer caused so much destruction? The caves. They were smarter than we thought. It was apparent from the drag marks that at least three had been coming back nightly to feast on the dead.

I had ducked into the sawmill tower and was seated on a log stump. It seemed out of place. I happily sat and looked through the window. My eyelids were heavy, and my chin bobbed against my chest. This was, perhaps, the first time I'd stopped moving in over twenty-four hours. Slapping my cheek, I blinked hard, shook my head, and sucked in a deep breath. As I slowly exhaled, I froze.

Yellow.

Not just yellow. Mustard yellow. The color of a lumberjack shirt.

It stuck out brightly against the evergreens and fall leaves.

They were here.

I stepped back, out to the top of the log flume, to get a better vantage point.

It occurred to me for a moment it could be a straggler from Crempshaw. A survivor. I squinted and followed the man with my tired eyes. No. No way. A survivor wouldn't be lurking in the scrub brush.

Then I spotted a colorful flannel shirt, and a blue one, and another. Paul was stupid. First, he alerted us with torches on the mountain. Now he hadn't even bothered dressing them in non-conspicuous-colored clothes. Idiot. Although, knowing him, he probably thought he'd catch us on the first day.

I signaled down to Marshall, waving my arms wildly until I got his attention. Adrenaline pulsed through my veins. It was go time. An odd feeling of excitement, fear, and anger churned inside me. We were as ready as we'd ever be. Everyone scattered to their various stations.

The brightly-colored shirts all congregated together with a few muted shirts I hadn't initially seen. They were huddled like a football team. Except this wasn't a game. I tried to count them, but they weren't still. My hands shook, and I resorted to pointing out each one and counting on my fingers. Fifteen, plus Paul. I think. Probably all mechanicals. I signaled down how many I'd seen. Hidden behind the pole, I was certain they hadn't spotted me.

Hands waving, fingers pointing, and frustrated yells were all I could make out. They were roughly a hundred yards away. They argued in muffled tones, but occasionally, I'd hear someone yell a word or two before lowering their voice. It seemed like they were fighting about breaking in. Crempshaw was bigger than I'd anticipated. I'm sure they thought the same thing.

One man pushed another, then a punch was thrown. A loud, fleshy smack followed. Paul broke up the fight and pushed forward.

"That's right," I whispered. My hands shook. Jitters. I stuffed them in my pockets for the moment. "Come here, Paul. Let's finish this."

They scurried to the gate like a bunch of rabid squirrels. Paul had a system of his own and threw up a hand signal. They all pushed on the gate at the same time. But the gate pushed back. So far, so good.

Despite the cold, my face was slick with sweat, my stomach did somersaults, and my heart raced. Suddenly, I wanted them to leave. We could run, live like gypsies. Just live. A loud chainsaw ripped through the crisp air. Gooseflesh broke out over my body. I shuddered.

Paul tore through the gate with his chainsaw arm with ease. The element of surprise was gone on their part. I signaled down to Marshall. *Hold your ground. Be ready.* The lumberjacks howled and yelled as Paul breached the gate. If they were trying to intimidate us, it was working.

After a few short minutes, Paul had made a hole large enough for them to enter. After Paul, fifteen bodies emerged through the newly minted entrance. Paul's foot was on the edge of the hole Frank had so carefully built and covered. Just a few scant inches and it could be over. *Yes. Step through, dear brother.*

Paul stiffened and raised his hand. The army stopped abruptly. The brush covering the hole shifted a tiny bit. I tensed.

Looking down at Paul was like looking in a mirror at a carnival. It was similar, but distorted enough to make you uncomfortable. He was my blood. But his blood was bad. Wrong somehow.

He lifted his lips into an evil smile.

"Annalise." He cupped his hands around his mouth. "Come out, come out, wherever you are!"

CHAPTER 53

The tips of their boots flirted with disaster. Just a few more inches and half of his soldiers would be lost. My stomach fluttered. I signaled for someone near the back to run across the back of camp, draw them in.

Paul raised his right arm. I stared at the disgusting chainsaw on his left arm. It pulled heavy on his shoulder. Even after all this time, his body hadn't fully adapted to the appendage. It was unnatural. His arm lingered for a moment before he let it fall.

The men rushed forward and around, scattering like rats. Three men lucked out and unknowingly circumvented the hole and ran deep into camp. Then, two fell into the pit. The remaining men near the entrance halted.

Screams of agony echoed. I peeked my head around the pole and snuck a glance at the pit. Crimson soaked the midsection of one man. A sharpened branch stuck out both sides of his body, suspending him in midair, his face frozen in shock.

Dead.

The other wasn't as lucky. Battered and bloodied, the thickest part of his femur was impaled. Bone jutted and blood pooled around him. He screamed desperately. I rubbed my calf. His voice quickly became raw, but he still cried out. If he'd hit his other leg, which was an ax, he would have been fine. But fate wasn't on his side.

The scent of iron-rich blood filled the air. Finally, the man stopped wailing.

Dead.

"Well done." Paul slowly clapped. "But I must wonder, is that the best you've got?"

I swallowed hard. Two down, fourteen to go.

"Annalise," he said in a singsong voice. He peered over the edge at his two fallen men. "Or should I say, *Angus*? Stephen told me everything. It turns out we shouldn't have followed your breadcrumbs to Camp Louvier. He was right all along. You were here at Crempshaw the whole time. You stole from me. My supplies, my blankets, but most importantly, my breeders." He bared his teeth, then grabbed a dark-haired man by his shoulders and stared at him. "Stephen, here, has been quite helpful. And for that, he shall be rewarded."

Paul used his right hand and pulled on his left arm as quick as lightning. A loud whir cut through the air. He zipped his arm across Stephen's gut.

From my vantage point, I couldn't see Stephen's face. But Paul's face, that I could see. Blood speckled his face and teeth. Was he smiling? His chainsaw arm hung limply, thick blood dripping onto the dirt.

Stunned, Stephen grabbed at his intestines as they erupted from his belly, and he staggered. Paul raised a boot and kicked him backward. I turned my head, but the sick, wet thud of his body landing in the pit was unmistakable.

I looked over to Frank. His neck muscles strained, and his jaw pulsed. I couldn't tell if he was mad at Stephen for betraying us or Paul for murdering his friend. It didn't matter. He needed to stay put, stick to the plan.

"No one!" Paul said. "No one betrays me! Not even in thought. Now, dear sister, come here and accept your *humane* punishment as Stephen received. Or wait and accept a worse fate. That goes for everyone," he screamed.

"Three down, thirteen to go," I whispered.

Paul paced slowly around the exposed hole, nine following him closely. The three mechanicals who'd made it around the hole preceded farther into camp cautiously.

I watched. Waited. Ready to signal my crew.

"Annalise," Paul sang quietly. "Annalise." He sang repeatedly, gaining volume each time. "Annalise!" he screamed. "Come fight me like a man! You wanted to be a man so badly, prove it. Enough with these games."

The corners of my lips formed into a smile. He was getting frustrated.

"Come fight me, you coward." Paul raised his arms.

My spine stiffened.

CHAPTER 54

Paul whistled. The three who'd run up ahead started destroying everything in their path. Anger thumped in my rib cage. They destroyed not only the things we'd fixed but also things that had gone unscathed. They were worse than the keringer.

Paul led his nine disciples to the bonfire in the middle of camp. "Annalise, I know you're here."

I looked over to Marshall. He stuck his head out of the sawmill kitty-corner from me, waiting for my signal. *Not yet.*

The mechanicals and Paul huddled around the fire. Probably planning my demise. Waving my hand in a circle, I gave the sign. Marshall nodded once and disappeared behind the sawmill.

The throttle sputtered a moment, and then the engine turned over. It was too loud—I heard it even from my side of camp. Startled, Paul and his men turned toward the noise. A six-foot saw blade rolled toward them.

It felt like it was all happening in slow motion. Like Paul had an eternity to move. But in reality, it was no more than fifteen seconds.

Most dove out of the way. One mechanical wasn't as lucky as the others who'd managed to move. His leg became separated from his body. Blood pooled around him as he lay on the ground panting. Tendons, muscle, and bone poked out from his thigh. If they were quick, they could tie it off and he might survive.

Two other mechanicals froze entirely. Stunned. The first was sliced vertically, right down the middle. His body split like two sides of a pistachio shell. The second man tried to move, but not quickly enough. The blade cut through his left arm, leg, and part of his head, severing them instantly. I sucked in a breath. The sound of metal ripping through skin, muscle, and bone tore through camp. Brains, blood, and intestines littered the ground like confetti at a potlach.

Crempshaw kept their blades much sharper than we did. It easily cut through them and continued on its path. Paul looked up at the sawmill, then whipped his head toward my log flume. Eyes full of hate. His head suddenly jerked to the left.

The saw had finally come to rest with a loud thud and lodged in the opposite wall. I made note of it. Maybe I could ram someone into it later.

Five down, one severely injured, ten to go.

CHAPTER 55

"Get him!" Paul yelled.

Two men rushed to the aid of the lumberjack with the severed leg. The first one whipped off his belt and used it as a tourniquet. The man writhed in pain as the belt tightened around his ruined appendage. They dragged him to the edge of camp. But it was a futile effort. The tourniquet wasn't tight enough, and blood flowed out of his body at an alarming rate. The man would likely bleed out in a matter of seconds.

Paul's face looked up toward the sky. His neck bulged and his face was bright red. His head dipped back, and he released a primal scream. Everyone stopped for a moment. His swollen eyes protruded from his head. All eyes were fixated on his next move.

"Enough," he finally said. "Finders keepers, losers weepers, Annalise." He scanned the area. "And you're going to lose!"

I clenched my fist and signaled to Tommy. Perched high on top of camp, he released a log on his pulley system. It careened at the line of men. They were like pins in a bowling alley. Unfortunately, they were ready. The pulley system shrieked under the weight. I watched Tommy doing his best to control the log as he pulled it toward him. He wavered momentarily, and almost fell off the top. Mechanicals jumped and lunged out of the way.

Damn it.

Not a single one was hit. The log slowed as it slammed against the side of the wall, sending a small tremor through camp.

Suddenly, three mechanicals walked from behind a building. They were the three who'd run up ahead. One man was holding a barely conscious Elizabeth. It was quite the juxtaposition. Frank had carried her in the same manner, but under much different circumstances. She had blood flowing from her lip. Her head wound was reopened and sputtered blood down her face. Her nose was bent to the side, and one eye was swollen shut. The three men didn't look much better. Even with a broken leg, she'd fought. But three against one? She didn't stand a chance. Her eyes fluttered a few times, and she was out. The slight movement in her chest gave me a bit of relief. She was alive.

For now.

"We got one, Lumberchief Paul," the mechanical yelled.

Camp grew silent.

Where was Paul? I searched the camp. I was too focused on Elizabeth and had lost sight of him.

Desperate to find him, I gave up my hiding spot and stuck my head out the window.

"What are you doing?" Marshall whispered below.

I jumped into the sawmill and looked down from my perch. At the bottom of the mill, logs waiting to be cut and sent down the flume were stacked on one side. I leaned over the ladder and stared at Marshall.

"I lost him," I said. "Go to the catapults, make sure our people are out of the way, and give Lillian the signal to fire when you deem fit." I jumped to my feet. My belly constricted. I leaned my head out the window and scanned Crempshaw again. "I have to find Paul. Where is he?"

My entire body went cold. The hairs on the back of my neck stood at attention. I lifted my head and looked to the far right corner. Diagonal from me, in the sawmill across camp, two icy-blue eyes, exactly like my own, stared at me.

Paul.

He mouthed something to me.

I knew that look. I knew that word. He'd mouthed it to me before.

It was the same one he'd given me when we would play hide-and-seek as kids. Before he changed, he was almost kind. Almost. When I picked an obvious spot, he'd mouth "gotcha," to me, close his eyes, and give me a second chance. Hiding had been a useful skill to learn.

I stared at him as he said the same word again. I read his lips.

Gotcha.

There would be no second chances today.

"Lumberchief," the man holding Elizabeth yelled. "They killed Val and Emerson. Sliced 'em right in half."

"Kill her." Paul never took his eyes off me.

"No!" I yelled. "Now, Lillian!"

To my left, two red-hot boulders flew through the air. Lillian had suggested setting a small fire centered under the rocks. It was brilliant. Even if the weight of the stone didn't kill them, the burn would.

There wasn't really any aim with the catapults. Even if there were, she couldn't see the commotion from where she was. But she could luck out, and at the very least it would give us some time to regroup. Create a diversion.

The boulders seemed to hang in the air for a minute. The mechanicals dove and tried to take cover. Two of the men rushed back into the building from which they emerged. The third dropped Elizabeth and ran for cover.

Frank ran by in a blur, scooped up Elizabeth as he'd done on our journey here, and ran out of sight. But this time, she didn't gasp with happy surprise. She was limp. Her chest no longer filled with air. Her skin was pallid. After all she'd been through, it appeared that she'd succumbed to her injuries.

Emotion welled up in my throat.

The first boulder struck the ground near the front of camp. My perch atop the log flume rattled. The second boulder slammed into the roof where Elizabeth's captors had run for safety. An explosion of wood splinters erupted from the impact. Smoke billowed out of the building as a fire broke out. It would likely go out on its own unless there was an accelerant in the building. But for now, it served its purpose.

They were trapped. Would burn to death or die of asphyxiation. Either way, I didn't care.

Eight down, eight to go.

CHAPTER 56

Throughout the chaos, Paul stared at me the entire time. Every time I looked at him, his gaze was fixed on his prey. I did my best to keep his location while watching the catapult's destruction. He'd moved so slowly, I didn't notice how close he'd crept to my location.

I scanned the area, my throat dry. The women, tall and short, fought the remaining seven mechanicals. We outnumbered them, but we were no match for their modified appendages. Heck, our group couldn't even get close enough to land a blow. They had an advantage, and if we didn't find a way to outsmart them, we were doomed.

Dead.

"Retreat!" I yelled. What happened? They were supposed to man their stations. What was the point of me giving orders if everyone was going to go rogue? How we ended up in a physical fight was a mystery to me. "Retreat!" They did as instructed, and disappeared behind structures and climbed up pulleys and sawmills.

"No," I said slowly. "No!" I yelled.

Frank had cornered himself. The seven remaining mechanical lumberjacks converged on him. Each displayed their grafted modification proudly. Whipping their axes in the air. Hammering the ground. Revving their chainsaws.

"Bring it," Frank yelled. Palms facing the sky, he wiggled his fingers, taunting them.

"Cowards," José yelled. He'd run back out from his station. "You think seven on one is a fair fight?" he spat. "You disgust me."

Doc emerged from the shadows, taking the heat off Frank. With a fairer fight, Frank stood a chance. The chainsaws wafted dirt from the ground into a fine mist and caused a dust storm. It became hard to make out the scene below. I squinted and continued to watch. Strategize. Plot. All while keeping an eye on Paul.

A lumberjack with a saw for an arm lunged at José. José leapt out of the way. From behind, another mechanical smashed the back of his head with a hammer. He was stunned. Lights on, no one's home. He wavered for a moment, then his knees buckled, blood and gray matter seeping down his shoulders. He crumpled to his knees, then onto the ground. His eyes went dark.

I bit my lip. José had survived the keringer attack, only to be murdered by a mechanical from Younish. And I'd led them here. I shook my head.

"Retreat," Doc yelled to Frank.

Doc ran but was confronted with the hammer-head mechanical. Blood ran down the hammer. José's blood. In a swift motion, Doc plunged a knife into the lumberjack's heart and fled the opposite direction. The mechanical fell forward, further embedding the knife into his heart.

Then I felt it.

That stare.

I looked wildly around, searching for those icy-blue orbs. His eyes grabbed mine like a bear in a trap. He stalked in my direction. A petite woman ran past him. He grabbed her by the hair and slit her gullet. Never breaking eye contact with me. Crimson flecks dotted his already blood-speckled face. Even with all the chaos, his face remained emotionless, calm.

Not knowing what else to do, I signaled up to Tommy. He nodded and swung another log down. A few mechanicals fell, and more importantly, it gave Frank and Doc a chance to run. Get back to their stations. Stick to the plan.

Paul continued to slink toward my sawmill.

I froze. He was too close.

I looked away and saw a blur in my periphery. All I could see was him disappearing beneath me. Inside my sawmill. I gasped. A crazed fox hunting his prey. Unpredictable.

Nine down. Seven to go.

CHAPTER 57

I stepped onto the perch in the sawmill and heard Paul rustling below, his chainsaw biting into anything in his path. I jumped back out onto the log flume and pulled at the string to release the stacked logs. It was my only chance out. My hand ripped open as I pulled. Blood soaked the rope; my hand slipped, shredding more skin. I cursed.

I was trapped. The constant whir of Paul's chainsaw only added to my frustration. I dipped back into the sawmill. Desperate, I kicked the ladder off its hinge. It landed with a thud. Paul laughed. I stepped back out, almost losing my balance, and pulled with everything I had. My skin tore further, my hand completely raw now. I leveraged my feet against the wood and pulled again. My back hitched. I screamed and was suddenly thrust back.

The logs finally budged.

They rolled with a roaring thunder. Before I could warn anyone, I heard an unsuspecting person crunch under the first log. With no time to spare, I launched myself down the flume. As I pushed off, I felt Paul's chainsaw narrowly miss my head and make contact with where my hair would have been. The scent of exhaust followed me down the flume.

The water soaked my backside and splashed my face

as I slid down the waterslide. It was so cold, it took my breath away. At the bottom, my momentum slowed just enough so I could jump out. A body lay sprawled, crushed into the ground. I closed my eyes and shook my head. If it was one of our own, that meant I had sacrificed their life for mine.

I raced toward the pulley system and never looked back. I wrapped my water-logged beanie around my cut hand and hoisted myself up. Paul slid down the flume. Pain seared through my palm as I climbed hand over hand, lugging my pregnant body toward safety high above the camp.

Once I was close, Tommy pulled me up the rest of the way, along with the rope. At the top of the wall, the wind blew against my heavy, wet clothes. My teeth chattered involuntarily, and my breath caught in the cold. I'd never felt cold like this before. But even so, I wasted no time, carefully running to the other side and lowering myself to Frank.

"Frank," I gasped. I was panting and my foggy breath hung in the air. "Can you go to the sawmill in the back?"

"Isn't that Marshall's station?" he asked.

"Yes," I said. "But I sent him to help Lillian launch the catapults. I don't know where he is now."

He nodded. "I know what to do." He ran along the edge toward the mill.

I pulled myself back up. With each pull, my hand throbbed in protest. It was amazing how an injury on such a small body part could be the difference between life and death. Once at the top, I sat on the flat surface of the fence to search for Paul. Younish had polished ours to a spike; I was thankful Crempshaw had not.

Camp was quiet. It smelled of soot and death. A small fire burned where the catapult had hit. Then I saw the log where I had accidently crushed someone. It was time for me to face the music. I squinted. Mangled metal was attached to the body. A mechanical. I rubbed my hand over my cold head, thankful I hadn't killed one of our own.

"Annalise," Paul called out. I couldn't see him. "Come see your brother. It's time we had a little chat."

"Screw you." I crouched as small as I could make myself. "We outnumber you, Paul."

"That's *Lumberchief* Paul!" he yelled.

"You'll never be my lumberchief—you're a sick, demented fraud."

"No matter." He stepped out into plain view. "I'll just talk to Marshall. The same way I *talked* to Walter." He held Marshall from behind, with his chainsaw up to his neck.

It felt like a knife had plunged into my heart. I'd long suspected him of Walter's murder, but now, he confirmed it. I had enough blood on my hands.

"No!" I yelled. "Don't you dare. Don't—don't hurt Marshall."

"Don't hurt Marshall," he mocked. "Don't you mean Marsh? Marsh, Marsh, Marsh. Marshall the liar." He released him and kicked him in the back. Marshall fell to his knees, hands bound behind him. "Marshall the thief!" He started up the chainsaw.

I grabbed the rope and jumped without a second thought. Paul was right, he was my Marsh. My sweet, wonderful, caring Marsh who had done everything for me. Volunteered to raise my baby. He was my future. *Our* future. Wind bit at my skin, but it didn't matter. I had my sights set directly on Paul. He had no time to react. I hit him at an angle and we both fell.

"Run," I said to Marshall before I even got to my feet. "Go now, you know what to do!"

Paul slowly stood. He licked blood from his swollen lip.

"Sister." He spat.

"Brother."

I crouched with my fists up, ready to fight. He mirrored me when I sidestepped but maintained the same distance. It was as if we were circling a boxing ring, sizing each other up, waiting for the opponent to land the first blow.

"You killed Walter." My voice faltered when I said his name.

"Of course I did." He bared his bloody teeth. "He wasn't fit to lead. Too soft. Treating everyone like equals."

I stared at the sawmill behind him and stopped. Again, he mirrored me and stood firmly in place.

"We're not equals. The superior shall reign, the weak must fall."

"Then why not let us go? You don't want us."

"Oh, Annalise, always such a dreamer." He splayed his arms out. "If I let you steal from me, rob me of my breeders, supplies, wagons, then word will get out. We'll have grifters pilfering our camp. Now, we can't have that."

"No one cares about your crappy camp, Paul," I said. "You're a murderer. He was my love. Your friend. The father of my baby! You killed Walter in cold blood."

"He was, wasn't he?" He tapped his finger on his chin. "Yes. He didn't see it coming, didn't suspect a thing. It was beautiful. I led him to the stream. The shallow one that only runs after a heavy rain fall. All it took was one hit to the back of the head to knock him down and stun him. Then I held his head under the water. He thrashed, kicked, and scratched desperately. Even gave me this little souvenir." He pulled his shirt down along his neck to reveal a pink scar. "I held him, stared into his confused eyes, until I saw the last bubble pop up. His body went limp. Then a simple turn of his body so he was facedown concealed my masterful art."

Pain blossomed in my chest. Heat flooded my body.

"And no one questioned it," Paul said proudly. "Everyone believed he got drunk and passed out, face first in the stream. Now it's your turn. You and that worthless parasite growing in you."

"Fine." I gritted my teeth. "Then give everyone a chance to leave. Let them go. Exchange myself and the *true* heir of Younish for them."

"Do you really think you have the upper hand here?"

"Do you?" I asked. My heart raced.

He raised his chainsaw arm, and it whirred to life. "I do."

"Do you think that scares me?" I clenched my fist above my head and swiftly brought it down. "And you're forgetting something."

"No, *you're* forgetting something." He lunged at me.

I held my spot as long as I could. Over Paul's shoulder, a six-foot saw barreled toward us. I took a step to the left and he followed. It shook the ground. He looked behind him. I jumped at the last moment.

Paul screamed. It was music to my ears.

Paul down. Five to go. No, none to go. The rest didn't matter.

We'd won.

I thought.

CHAPTER 58

Paul stood, holding his mangled left arm.

"What? Shit!" I jumped to my feet. "How?"

"Look what you've done," Paul yelled. His chainsaw arm had been severed by the circular saw, but the rest of him was unscathed. Blood seeped, and wires sparked and zapped. "What have you done?" He pointed to the demolished saw on the ground. "It was a perfect fit." His words were confident, but his voice was strained, face red. He was in pain.

"Pauly," I said. I hadn't called him that since we were kids. "Oh, Pauly, I'm so sorry. "Are you okay?" I picked up the broken chainsaw and rushed over to him.

"A–Annalise?" His face contorted with disgust. "What are you doing?"

"We'll get you a new one." I could smell the blood and guts on his clothes. "I can't believe I almost killed you. You're my brother. Family. You're going to be an uncle. I'm sorry. I'm so sorry. Here." I handed him the saw. "Take it."

With his right hand, he slapped it away. The chain bit at my arms. I gripped at something smooth in my pocket.

"What is this?" He waved for his mechanicals to assist. "What are you doing? Have you lost your mind?"

"Maybe a little." I held out my free hand in surrender.

"Yes, you have." Paul raised his right arm and backhanded me.

I swallowed and breathed hard through my nostrils but didn't react.

"You thought you could beat me? My men?! Real men. Not like you. A silly scrawn pretending to be a lumberjack—"

"I'm not a lumberjack." I spat blood. "You're right."

"Finally, you admit defeat." Paul grasped a hatchet from his belt.

"Lumberjill!" I screamed. "I'm a lumberjill!" I lunged.

The keringer saber-fang sank into his neck. The flesh broke, and I pushed harder. His muscles ripped and spasmed, blood pooling around the edges. Fibers broke, veins serrated. I yanked it out and stabbed him again. An unsettling smile formed on my face. His warm blood splattering on my face felt like a welcome rain shower in the dead of summer. I released my grip, leaving the tooth impaled in his neck. The mother keringer had saved us.

Paul staggered back, his eyes wide, clutching his neck. He pawed at the fang with his right hand, perhaps in the same fashion Walter had while Paul drowned him. He coughed a wet gurgle. Pink froth formed at the corners of his lips. Blood sprung from his mouth. Finally, he fell to the ground, and he stared at me, those icy-blue eyes penetrating me again.

I crouched next to him and lowered my mouth to his ear. "Aw, don't die too quickly. I have an announcement." I stood. "The lumberchief of Younish has been released!"

CHAPTER 59

My entire body shook. I reached down and gripped the bloody fang lodged in my brother's neck. I jerked it, and blood drained from his dead body.

"I earned this." I gritted my teeth. The world spun and my vision clouded.

Marshall's hand clasped my shoulder. "Anna." He turned me to face him.

"I'm fine," I said to him. "I am."

I turned and retched.

"Sorry."

"At least it wasn't on my shoes this time," Marshall said. "What do we do with the rest of the mechanicals?"

"Round them up."

I walked over to the fire and sat. The smell of burning wood replaced the lingering death. I wrung my shaking hands in a futile attempt to wipe them clean. Coming into this, I'd known what I had to do. And when faced with it, I hadn't backed down. But now, a small bit of regret crept up. Maybe I was as bad as my brother. I couldn't help but wonder if the same darkness that flowed through his veins was also in mine.

Everyone gathered around the fire. Some were worse for the wear, but at least they were alive. Adrenaline waned and emotions erupted. Some were crying; others sat listlessly. Reality set in. We'd won, but our future was still uncertain.

"Annalise," Frank said.

I raised my head.

Tommy and Doc led five bound and injured mechanicals toward us. Three were missing their ax arms, one was limping with a stick—his mechanical leg missing, and the last one had a gaping hole in his head where a hammer had been. All were shirtless.

"Tommy!" I said.

"I did the fighting. Doc did the tying."

"What now?" Lillian said.

"I don't know." I stood. "What should we do?"

"Don't know what to do?" Hazel asked. "What was your plan all along, Annalise?"

"I just wanted to save us," I said.

"You brought us this far," Frank said. "You saved the women and defeated Paul. You know what has to be done."

"Frank . . ." I started. He was right, but I couldn't say it.

"No, no." Frank held up his hands defensively. "Let me carry this burden. Not you."

I nodded once and immediately turned away.

"No," one of the mechanicals protested. "Please, it was a mistake." Anger that I'd saved for Paul reared its ugly head.

"Mistake!" I screamed. "Killing innocent women and *babies* was a mistake?"

"We didn't kill them babies," the mechanical said. "Their mothers did."

The other four nodded and agreed.

That was all I needed to hear. They still didn't get it. Women, at their most vulnerable time in their lives, forced to give birth in front of a crowd. All the while knowing what was next. Their hand forced into an iron fist wielding an ax until they could no longer support it. The horror they must have felt as their arms gave way. The feeling of the ax connecting with their newborn's neck.

Still, they took no responsibility.

And worse, they didn't see the errors of their ways.

"Thank you, Frank." My nostrils flared.

"No!" the mechanicals yelled.

Frank, Tommy, and Doc led them toward a sawmill.

The men fought and kicked but were no match. Tommy held them at ax-point, and Doc poked them with a stick, moving them forward.

"Ugh," Hazel said. "I am not watching this."

"I am." I put my hands on my hips. "They humiliated and murdered Jeanette and Ruby before our eyes. Don't they deserve the same?"

"I—" Hazel said.

"Do what you want. All of you," I said. "But for me? I need the closure."

"Everyone must do what is right for them," Patricia said. "We all process and heal differently, I suppose."

I turned and watched Frank lead them to the top of the mill. Ropes around their necks led back into the open window—anchored to the engine inside, I assumed. They stood on the ledge. I heard their pleas but felt nothing. Frank pushed them, one by one, off the ledge. Sawdust plumed each time, creating a dusty filter. But I still saw them dangling. Two of them kicked wildly for what felt like an eternity, then remained still. The other three were lucky, and death met them with a broken neck.

I felt a shiver. I scanned the area and realized everyone

else was by the fire. I waited for Frank, Doc, and Tommy and walked with them to rejoin the group.

"It is done," Frank said to the group.

"I guess we should get this place secure before night-fall," Tommy said.

Regardless of how tired we were, no one protested.

Once the gate and all holes were fixed, we spent the rest of the day burying the dead. A peaceful cemetery was created far away from Crempshaw's walls. I bowed my head and placed a pine bough on my brother's grave. I knew I should have cried, but my eyes remained dry. I wasn't sorry.

Nightfall came and we all settled into bed without dinner. Too tired to eat, really. Marshall settled in beside me.

"Anna." He stroked my stubbly head. "Do you think the others from Younish will be back?"

"I don't know. I doubt it. Someone else will be happy to be the leader once they don't return. They're all pow-er-hungry morons."

"What happens now?" Marshall asked.

I turned on my side and faced him. "Now? You have to live up to your promise."

"What's that?"

"Help me raise this baby."

"Anna . . ." His eyes filled tears.

"What?" I bit my lip

Marshall gently cradled my face in his hands. "I love you, Anna."

The emotion I'd kept buried deep inside me erupted. Tears streamed down my face—hard. There was no deny-ing it. I pressed my face into his shoulder and cried harder than I had in months.

"Anna?" Marshall whispered.

"I know you do." I wiped my tears and pressed my forehead against his. "I want to love you. It's just—I don't deserve you. You're too good for me. You're wonderful, thoughtful, kind, and everything I'm not."

"Then I guess it's a good thing I'll be around to help you with this baby, isn't it?" He held the nape of my neck and stared deep into my eyes.

"Thanks, Marsh," I said. "You make me feel safe. I don't know what I'd do without you."

"I know," he said. "You're a mess."

I hesitated, then tilted my head toward him and placed my lips against his. He put a hand on my lower back and pulled me closer. Electricity pulsed through my veins. I ran my fingers through his hair and breathed him in. My heart raced. I could have kissed him forever.

Marshall pulled back and stared into my eyes. "But you're *my* mess."

THE END

As a kid, Tyler H. Jolley always had a knack for storytelling. When he grew bored of old fables, he created his own exciting and unique worlds. Many years later, he still had so many new ideas and stories swirling in his head, but with nowhere to share it. That's when he put his pencil to paper and let the creative juices flow.

His debut novel, *Extracted*, came out in 2013 and swiftly became an Amazon Best Seller and Spencer Hill Press Best Seller. *Prodigal and Riven*, the second and third books in The Lost Imperials series were released in May of 2015.

After a brief hiatus he restructured and returned to writing. His Adventurous Ali series has received much praise. To date, he's released three in the series.

When he's not writing, you can find him at his orthodontic practice, mountain biking, or on the hunt for the perfect doughnut.